Large Print Geo
George, Catherine.
The temptation trap

WITHDRAWN

STACKS
MAR 1199

EU

THE TEMPTATION TRAP

THE TEMPTATION TRAP

BY

CATHERINE GEORGE

MILLS & BOON®

First published in Great Britain 1998
Large Print edition 1999
Harlequin Mills & Boon Limited,
Eton House, 18-24 Paradise Road,
Richmond, Surrey TW9 1SR

© Catherine George 1998

ISBN 0 263 15846 2

Set in Times Roman
16-9901-47806 C16½-18

Printed and bound in Great Britain
by Antony Rowe Ltd, Chippenham, Wiltshire

CHAPTER ONE

THE dark attic was airless in the heat of the June day. Rosanna swung herself up through the hatch, found the light switch and picked her way gingerly through boxes and bundles, past her brother's electric guitar and old tennis racquets, the small desk she'd used as a child. Eventually, behind a pile of boxes full of Christmas decorations, Rosanna spotted some battered old luggage and in triumph seized on a suitcase stencilled with the initials R.N. She threw open the lid, then sat back on her heels, suddenly reluctant to disturb the layers of silver paper. Her grandmother had been dead for a long time but it felt like trespass, nevertheless, to rummage through the belongings Rose Norman had once locked away so carefully.

In silent apology Rosanna lifted the top layers of paper, revealing not, as she'd expected, a favourite ballgown from Rose's youth, but worn grey dresses folded with voluminous

5

aprons yellow with age, the red cross prominent on the bibs.

Rose Norman had been a VAD, a member of the Voluntary Aid Detachment in the First World War. Rosanna had always loved hearing how her grandmother had left home at the tender age of seventeen to tend the wounded, unpaid, armed with only a basic training in first aid, but fired with the desire to help.

Rosanna took the clothes out and began filling polythene bags with the countless letters and photographs stored underneath. When the only thing left was a linen bag containing a rosewood box, Rosanna slid it into one of her carrier bags, replaced the clothes in the case, then climbed down to the landing with her haul and pushed the stairs up into place behind their square wooden cover in the ceiling.

Rosanna took her treasure trove down to the kitchen and laid it out on the big round table, amused by her mother's cunning. Rosanna had actually been driving her to Heathrow Airport when Henrietta Carey casually mentioned that a man was coming to the house the following evening.

'I meant to tell you before, darling, but with you so snowed under with work it slipped my mind. This Mr Fraser called round last week, credentials very much in order. I thought you wouldn't mind dealing with it.'

'Deal with what? Who is he? What does he want?'

Mrs Carey explained that quite by chance she'd seen an item in the Personal column of *The Times*, a request for information about Miss Rose Norman.

'Really?' Rosanna's eyes lit up. 'Why didn't you tell me this before?'

'I thought you might talk me out of contacting Mr Fraser in case he was up to no good.'

'As if I could talk *you* out of anything!' Rosanna chuckled and, having parked the car, began hauling out suitcases. 'Who is he, and where does Grandma come in?'

'He's involved in research for memoirs of some kind. I liked him.' Henrietta gathered up her flight bag, smiling at her daughter. 'I told him to call round after dinner, so make sure you're in.'

Rosanna drove back into North-West London, quite taken by the idea of research about Rose Norman. Henrietta Carey hadn't enlarged much on this Mr Fraser, but if he was writing memoirs he was obviously elderly. In which case, after sherry and biscuits, and some reminiscences about her grandmother, he could be eased politely on his way. In the meantime, thought Rosanna happily, with no Monday morning rush to work she had an entire, leisurely day to sort something out for this Mr Fraser.

Rosanna had assumed she knew everything there was to be known about her grandmother, until her mother mentioned the suitcase. Rose Norman had passed it on to her daughter just before she died, and told her to show it to Rosanna when the time was right.

And now, thought Rosanna, pulling the first batch of letters towards her, the time is perfect. She'd packed in her job and, though sharing a flat with her friend Louise was fun most of the time, the prospect of living alone for a while, house-sitting for her mother, was absolute bliss. A spot of research about young VAD Rose Norman was the icing on the cake.

Rosanna forced herself to leave the rosewood box locked for the time being. It so obviously contained something special, she would save it for last. The rest of the papers were mainly letters and cards from members of the family, along with photographs of Rose's parents and her sister Amelia, stiff, posed portraits very different from the bundles of amateurish family snapshots of a later date.

Rosanna quickly sorted letters and photographs into date order before settling down to read the diaries, which gave a fascinating insight into the life of the time. She read of Gerald Rivers' proposal, and how dashing he looked in his officer's uniform. Rose had accepted him, and he'd kissed her reverently and gone off to war, and that was the last she'd seen of him.

'Gerald is dead,' said a final, terse entry in 1916. 'I cannot stay here, grieving and idle. There must be some way to make myself useful.'

At that point Rosanna found she couldn't keep her eyes open. She yawned wearily, then locked up for the night, deciding to leave the rosewood box for the morning.

Next day Rosanna was so deeply affected after reading the contents of the box, she went for a long run in the park in the early evening, and only just managed to make herself presentable by the appointed hour. In deference to the probable age of her visitor she borrowed a linen skirt and white voile blouse of her mother's, and used only a minimum of make-up, and was still piling her damp hair into a knot on top of her head when the doorbell rang. She raced downstairs, tucking in escaping damp tendrils, threw open the door, then stared blankly at the man standing in the porch.

This was no elderly gentleman. He was tallish, with high cheekbones in a suntanned face, and a mop of thick black hair in need of a barber. And at a guess he was a mere few years older than she was. And equally surprised—dumbfounded even. He wore a light tweed jacket with jeans, polished loafers and a plain white T-shirt. And something about him was familiar. And very, very attractive. As she met the dazed look in his slanted eyes Rosanna stiffened, astounded by a deep-down flicker of reaction. And as though he sensed it he moved towards her involuntarily, then stopped dead, the hand he'd half raised dropping to his side again.

'Good evening,' he said huskily at last. He cleared his throat. 'My name's Fraser.'

'Hello,' said Rosanna, pulling herself together. 'My mother said you were coming tonight.'

'Would you like proof of my identity?' He produced a yellow card with a photograph and signature that confirmed he was E. A. Fraser, a member of the National Union of Journalists. 'If you want confirmation your best bet at this time of night would be the offices of the *Sunday Mercury*.'

'Is that where you work?'

'Not any more. But I'm well-known there. Someone would vouch for me.'

Rosanna shook her head, telling herself she'd imagined that first, startled moment of rapport. 'I don't think that's necessary. I gather you've already met my mother. Do come in.' She smiled, determinedly polite, and held out her hand. 'I'm Rosanna Carey.'

Her visitor shook her hand formally, then followed her along the hall to a small sitting room, where French windows opened on a long, narrow garden at the back of the house.

'Thank you for seeing me, Miss Carey.' His careful formality belied the look in his eyes, which were still riveted to her face. 'Your mother told me she had some papers I could borrow.'

'Quite a lot of them. I did some rummaging in the attic for you.' Rosanna made no mention of her mother's holiday. Bad idea to say she was living temporarily and alone in the house. 'My mother couldn't be here this evening. She asked me to deputise for her.'

'It's very kind of you.' Her visitor looked away at the garden at last, breathing in appreciatively as the scent of roses came wafting in on the warm evening air. Someone was mowing a lawn nearby, and there were faint shouts from children playing in a garden a few houses away. 'This is very pleasant. I miss a garden.'

'Do sit down. Can I offer you a drink?' Rosanna smiled, her eyes dancing suddenly. 'I had sherry and biscuits lined up. I thought you'd be nearer my grandmother's age than mine.'

He smiled, his teeth gleaming white in his tanned face. 'Sorry to disappoint you.'

'Relieved, not disappointed,' she assured him lightly. 'I'd braced myself for a formal exchange with someone venerable. Though I'd better make it clear at the outset that I've got reservations about passing on some of the things I found.'

'Letters?' he asked quickly.

She nodded. 'Very private ones.'

He eyed her thoughtfully for a moment, then got to his feet. 'Look, could we go out for a drink? Miss Carey, you don't know me from Adam. So just to reassure you I'm not about to nick the silver I vote we adjourn to neutral ground while I ask my questions.'

'Are you writing some kind of article?' asked Rosanna curiously.

'No. This is nothing to do with any newspaper.' He took a book from his briefcase and handed it to her.

Rosanna looked at the cover, eyebrows raised. '*Savage Dawn*, by Ewen Fraser,' she noted, and turned to the back cover to look at a photograph of the author. Ewen Fraser. Of course. That was why his face was familiar. His book was a runaway bestseller. She'd read quite a lot about him recently. And not just about his books. 'No wonder I thought I knew you.'

'You've read it?' he said, pleased.

She shook her head. 'Sorry, I haven't. But you've been in the news lately. One way and another,' she added deliberately. Candid camera shots of Ewen Fraser, usually with some gorgeous female in tow, had appeared regularly in the press since his book made the bestseller list.

His wide, expressive mouth twisted in distaste. 'Don't believe everything you read, Miss Carey—other than my book, of course. That was researched with great care,' he said shortly, obviously nettled by her reference to his private life. '*Savage Dawn* is set in the Zulu wars. It's selling so well my editor wants a follow-up with a descendant in the same military family in the First World War. Which is why I'm interested in anything you can tell me about your grandmother.'

Rosanna frowned. 'Why *my* grandmother?'

'If you'll come and have a drink with me I'll explain.'

She thought for a moment. It was easy to see women, her mother included, took to Ewen Fraser on sight. Rosanna couldn't ignore the fact that she'd reacted the same way herself. Which was a first. 'All the necessary papers and records are here, Mr Fraser. We could hardly go through them in a pub. If you'll settle for a drink here we can go through the papers in peace.'

The leap of pleasure in his eyes ignited a second little flicker of heat inside her, to her consternation. 'I'd like that very much,' he said with emphasis. 'Thank you for sparing me the time.'

Rosanna took a quick look at her father's drinks supply. 'You don't look like a sherry type to me. Whisky? Brandy?'

Ewen Fraser smiled. 'Any hope of a beer, please?'

Rosanna went off to the kitchen, relieved to find the fridge yielded up a couple of cans of her father's favourite bitter. She collected a tankard, found some nuts and put them in a dish on a tray, added a tonic water for herself, then went back to her guest.

Ewen Fraser's manners were too good to plunge into immediate discussion of the reason for his visit. He told Rosanna he lived in Chelsea, and that the idea for his best-selling novel had come from a series of articles he'd done for the *Mercury* on famous military heroes. While still working as a journalist he'd written two previous novels, but *Savage Dawn* was his first bestseller, and these days he wrote full-time. Rosanna, in return, told him she was a teacher, and shared a basement flat in Bayswater with a friend.

'Where do you teach?' he asked.

'I started out at a small, private school, re-placing someone on maternity leave. After that I was lucky enough to get a junior post at my old school, but it meant an academic year to fill in, so up to Easter I did some supply teaching. Along the way I did a course in computers and word-processing.' She smiled at him. 'Technology comes in handy these days.'

'I'm impressed,' he said, raising his tankard to her. 'So what are you doing until the autumn term? Holiday?'

She shook her head. 'An old college friend started up on his own last year. He works from home and argued it would hone my computer skills if I gave him a hand for a bit, so like a fool I agreed.'

'You obviously regret it.'

Rosanna's eyes kindled. 'Charlie Clayton wants a slave, not a secretary. He's an insolvency accountant, needs everything documented—not that I mind that part. But his wife goes out to work in the City every day, so Charlie expects me to provide coffee all the time, make him lunch, go shopping sometimes, even iron a shirt in an emergency.'

Her visitor's eyes gleamed with amusement. 'The last straw, obviously. Is that what you've been doing today?'

'No. The Claytons went off on holiday last week. Thank goodness. The workload up to that point was so heavy I decided it just wasn't on for the money he's paying me. I told Charlie that, but I don't think he believed me. When he gets back he can find another dogs-body—or get some voice-activated software and make his own lunch.'

'Good for you,' he approved.

'Help yourself to the other beer, Mr Fraser,' said Rosanna politely.

'Thank you. But I'd enjoy it more if you called me Ewen.'

'Then I will—you don't sound very Scottish,' she added.

'I'm sort of London Scottish,' he informed her. 'My father met my mother here when he first came down from Edinburgh to join a Fleet Street daily.'

'Ah! Printer's ink runs in your veins, then!' Rosanna drained her glass then got down to business. 'Right then, Ewen Fraser,' she said briskly, looking at him squarely. 'I've told you why I was surprised at the sight of you. But why, exactly, were you so thunderstruck at the sight of *me*?'

His attractive smile lifted one corner of his mouth. 'I thought I was seeing things. I know your grandmother's photograph very well. You're so like her you took my breath away.'

Rosanna stared, astonished. 'How on earth did you come by a photograph of my grand-mother?'

His eyes, set slantwise beneath ruler-straight brows, held hers. 'My great-uncle met Miss Rose Norman in France.'

'Ah, I see!' Rosanna leaned forward eagerly. 'Was he 2nd Lieutenant Henry Manners of the Royal Welch Fusiliers, by any chance?'

Ewen nodded. 'That's the one. Military Cross and Bar, DSO. By some miracle he managed to survive the war. He was a great old boy, a career soldier. Brigadier by the end. I was very fond of him.'

'Did he ever marry?'

He shook his head. 'No prizes for guessing why.'

'Because Miss Rose Norman married some-one else,' she said quietly.

They looked at each other in silence for a moment, then Rosanna got up. 'Let's make a start. We'll have to work at the kitchen table.'

Ewen leapt to his feet. 'Right. I haven't brought much. There's a huge amount at home, of course, but where your grand-mother's concerned it's just a diary, plus some letters and the photograph.'

'The same for me, too,' she said. 'I'm not counting the letters from relatives. The prize was a rosewood box left to my mother.' She smiled. 'I'd never seen it until yesterday. I made myself go through the other stuff first before opening it.'

When they were ready to start, Ewen dis-carded his jacket and drew his chair next to Rosanna's. She turned the small brass key in the lock of the rosewood box, then handed it to Ewen. He stared down at the photograph of Lieutenant Harry Manners, in uniform but hat-less, the grenades of the Royal Welch Fusiliers on his collar. His thick dark hair was combed flat, and his slanted eyes shone with bright certainty in his young, intelligent face.

'The letters are all from him,' said Rosanna quietly, suddenly conscious of Ewen's bare brown arm close to her own, of the fine hair which showed dark against his gold watch on a slim, sinewy wrist. She pulled herself together hurriedly. 'I'd rather you took them home and read them at your leisure,' she told him. Harry's letters were so passionate they were best read in private.

'Thank you. I'll leave Rose's letters for you.' Ewen pulled a leather box from the briefcase he'd brought, and pushed it towards her. And there, on top, was a photograph of Rose Norman in her bloom, a study her granddaughter had never seen before. Waving dark hair piled high, bare shoulders wreathed in white tulle, Rose Norman smiled with a radiance undimmed by the sepia tint of the photograph.

Rosanna swallowed a great lump in her throat. 'That smile,' she said huskily, 'was for Harry.'

Ewen nodded. 'I know. At first I felt like a voyeur, but once I started reading her letters I was hooked. I just had to know what happened. Damn silly, really. I knew perfectly well there was no happy ending, but I wanted one. Badly.'

'I know just what you mean. It felt like trespass when I opened Grandma's trunk yesterday.' Rosanna sighed. 'Her diary cut me to pieces in places. Harry Manners was obviously the love of her life. And by his letters she was very much his, too.'

'And yet she married your grandfather.'

Rosanna nodded, her eyes sombre. 'Yes.'

Ewen pushed his chair away slightly so he could turn to look at her. 'You resemble her so closely it's a pity old Harry never met you. And yet not. It would probably have been too painful for him.'

'You think I really look like that?' she said doubtfully, eyeing the photograph.

'You're her image,' he assured her, looking at her so objectively she suddenly felt jealous, stung by the idea that it was Rose he was seeing. Not Rosanna Carey, her flesh-and-blood grandchild.

'There's a fleeting similarity, I suppose,' she said, so furious with herself her tone was distant, and Ewen got up, quick to sense her change of mood.

'I've taken up too much of your time. If I could use your phone I'll call a cab.'

'Of course. There's a list of numbers on the hall table.'

After Ewen made the call he came back into the kitchen. 'May I take your box with me? I promise to take care of it. Or if you prefer I could just take the contents—'

'No. Keep the letters in it, but I'll keep the diary until tomorrow. You can have it then, when you go through the other things. There are later photographs of Rose, and letters to her from her family, and newspaper cuttings.' Rosanna preceded him into the hall to wait for the taxi. 'The cuttings are mostly about military events. Rose must have been following Harry's career.'

Ewen put the rosewood box in his briefcase. 'I'll go through these tonight, and bring it back as soon as possible. Is tomorrow any good? Would your mother mind if I came round in the evening? Or will you be back in your own place by then?'

Rosanna hesitated. 'A friend's using my room in the flat because I'm house-sitting,' she said reluctantly. 'My father's been away for the past month, doing consulting work in Saudi Arabia. My mother's gone to meet up with him at my brother's place in Sydney.'

'Australia.' He looked at her levelly. 'You were afraid to tell me that before.'

'Of course I was. I didn't know you!'

'You do now.'

'Do I?' she countered lightly.

'Of course you do, Miss Carey.' Ewen took her by the hand, turning her to face the large mirror on the wall. 'We're the descendants of two people who loved each other with a very grand passion indeed,' he told her reflection. 'We could hardly fail to know each other. Besides, having seen the portrait of Rose, I knew *you* the moment I set eyes on you.'

Rosanna eyed his reflection analytically. 'You don't look much like Harry.' She smiled a little. 'But I feel I know him a lot better than you.'

'Why?'

'I've read his letters!'

Ewen turned her to face him. 'Thank you for giving up your evening, Rosanna.'

He retained her hand, and Rosanna stood very still, her pulse quickening as his thin, strong fingers closed over hers. 'I enjoyed it. I've never met a celebrity before,' she said brightly.

He shrugged, his smile more crooked than before. 'No celebrity. Just a journalist who got lucky.' He looked down at her intently. 'I'll bring the letters back tomorrow night, then.'

Rosanna nodded, wishing he'd release her hand. 'All right.'

'This time have dinner with me.'

She shook her head. 'I don't think so, thank you.'

'I see.' Ewen dropped her hand. 'Right. I'll call round after dinner, then. Or before. Whatever.'

His expression was suddenly so aloof, Rosanna felt chilled. But not enough to agree to a meal together. She never accepted dinner invitations. Nor wanted to. But to her aston-

ishment she wanted to go out with Ewen
Fraser so much she had to force herself to refuse. 'After dinner. If you like,' she added casually.

The warmth returned to his eyes so suddenly
it kick-started her pulse again. 'I do like. Very
much. Tomorrow at eight-thirty, then.'

'Come a bit earlier than that—if you want
to get to grips with the other stuff, I mean,'
added Rosanna gruffly, and bit her lip.

Ewen grinned. 'Men usually beg *you* for
more time, of course, not the other way round.'

'I wasn't *begging*,' she said indignantly.

'I know.' He picked up his briefcase. 'You
just want to get everything finished and be rid
of me.' His eyes danced, the overhead hall
light picking out flecks of gold in the hazel
irises. 'I'd be here at nine in the morning if I
thought you'd let me in.'

This time the flicker of response was so vi-
olent Rosanna was hard put to hide it, and almost told him not to come again. But she
couldn't think of a feasible excuse, and her
tone was cold in sheer self-defence as she told

him seven-thirty in the evening would do very well.

Ewen smiled with regret as the doorbell rang. 'My cab. Goodnight, Rosanna.'

'Goodnight.' She opened the front door. 'Don't stay up late reading Harry's letters. In fact, take my advice—read them tomorrow, not tonight.'

'Why?'

She smiled wryly. 'You'll find out when you read them!'

CHAPTER TWO

FEELING oddly restless after Ewen Fraser had gone, Rosanna took her grandmother's letters to bed to read, which was a big mistake. In their own way the letters were as innocently erotic as the outpourings Rose Norman had received from Harry Manners.

Rosanna already knew how the two young people had met from the entries the young VAD had made in her diary. Rose Norman had been sent to France. With a couple of girl drivers for company, sometimes only one, she travelled in the unwieldy old ambulances of the time to transfer the seriously injured from casualty clearing stations to base hospitals further away from the front line.

2nd Lt. Harry Manners, one arm in a sling, a stained bandage round his forehead, flagged down Rose's ambulance one day to beg transport for two of his wounded men. The men were crammed in somehow, at which point a flat tyre was discovered. Rose managed to help Letty Parker, the driver, change the tyre with instructions from the young platoon commander, who promptly collapsed in an unconscious heap the moment they finished the job.

Between them the girls managed to heave him into the front seat, Rose holding him as upright as possible on the journey back to the base hospital. Harry Manners' forehead had been grazed by one sniper's bullet, and his shoulder pierced by another which missed the jugular vein and the spine by a hair's breadth, a 'Blighty' wound which sent him back to England to recover.

Fate sent Rose Norman home on leave on the same train, helping with the wounded on the journey. When she came across Harry he was light-headed and obviously feeling wretched, but utterly delighted to see her again. They were able to talk only briefly, but Harry begged her home address, and the moment he was discharged from the hospital in Denmark Hill called to see Rose on a day when her mother was helping Rose's sister,

Amelia, with the children's measles in Kensington.

Far into the night Rosanna lay in the same bedroom her grandmother had occupied as a girl, riveted by the account of a love affair all the more passionate and poignant for the modest, unaffected style of Rose Norman's letters. Referring to the diary from time to time, Rosanna read how Harry cut short his stay with his parents, and saw Rose every day, courtesy of the measles which focussed her mother's attention away from her younger daughter.

When Harry asked her to marry him, Rose, still shadowed by the loss of one fiancé, was superstitious, and implored him to wait until the war was over.

'But in the meantime,' wrote Rose, 'we are madly, wildly in love, and *alive.*

'Today,' said the next entry succinctly, 'we became lovers.'

The diary was blank after that until Rose arrived back in France, not earlier than scheduled due to curtailed leave, 'as she told her mother, but on the due date after a week of illicit bliss with Harry in a Brighton hotel.

Their next meeting was in France, when Rose managed to get time off to stay with Harry in a *pension* in Rouen before he went up to the front. When they parted Harry gave his love a brooch in the shape of a gold rose, and kissed Rose's tears away when she sobbed in his arms.

Rosanna slept late the following morning, and woke to a feeling of guilt. Overnight she'd had time for regrets, very much aware that there was no real necessity for Ewen to bring back the papers in person. Any future dealings with him could have been done by post. But she liked him. In fact, after just one meeting she felt as though she'd known Ewen for years. Or in some other life. Which was dangerous. It stemmed from Harry and Rose, of course. Their love story had fostered an intimacy that would never have happened if she'd met Ewen in other circumstances.

Ewen Fraser was an attractive, intelligent man loaded with charm. But, Rosanna reminded herself, apart from his great-uncle and his success as a writer she knew very little about him. Women, if the press were to be believed, flocked around Ewen Fraser in droves. For all she knew he might even be married. Not that it was any concern of hers if he had a wife or an entire harem.

The day was hot, and Rosanna spent most of it in the garden, topping up her tan. And later, after a quick salad supper, she took time with her appearance, choosing clothes that would show off her newly acquired glow. Some of which, she realised, eyeing her reflection, wasn't entirely due to the sun. She'd left her hair to lie loose and glossy on her shoulders, and in sharp contrast with the demure look of the night before wore a sleeveless pink shirt and brief denim skirt. Knowing she looked her best heightened anticipation hard to control as she went downstairs to wait for Ewen Fraser.

He arrived punctual to the minute, dressed in a thin white cotton shirt and pale khakis, and presented Rosanna with a bunch of roses, making no attempt to hide the pleasure he took at the sight of her.

'Hello, Rosanna. You look different with your hair down.' He smiled and handed over the flowers. 'Your garden's probably full of these, but nothing else seemed suitable.'

'Why, thank you. How kind.' Rosanna's smile masked the now familiar leap in her blood. 'I've been lazing in the garden. Would you like a drink out there before we tackle any more papers?'

Ewen agreed with alacrity, and Rosanna sent him off to sit in a garden chair while she put the roses in water. She took her time, breathing in their heady scent, feeling light-headed. There was no mistake, after all. During the day she'd tried to convince herself that Ewen Fraser was just a pleasant, rather clever young man, but nothing out of the or-dinary. One look at him again tonight had scotched that theory. He wasn't handsome ex-actly, but his tall, rangy body and slanted gold eyes were just as appealing on second acquain-tance as at first. Ordinary he was not. Rosanna went out into the garden with Ewen's beer, and sat down in one of the other deck chairs.

'You read the letters?' she asked at once, to emphasize that they were here for a purpose.

'Yes. I couldn't resist reading them last night after all,' he said ruefully. 'I couldn't get to sleep for hours. They were a revelation. Harry's love for Rose was blazingly physical, yet at the same time it's plain he absolutely worshipped her.'

'It was mutual.' Rosanna touched the gold rose pinned to the lapel of her shirt. 'This is the brooch he gave her in Rouen, the last time they saw each other.'

Ewen leaned closer to examine the pin, close enough for Rosanna to breathe in the scent of expensive soap and healthy male, and she moved away instinctively. He drew back at once, and for a moment there was an awkward silence. They broke it at the same time, then stopped and laughed a little.

'You first,' said Rosanna.

Ewen breathed in deeply. 'I was about to say I've already done the major part of the research—war records, and historians and war poets of the time. But Harry's diaries and the letters he wrote to Rose are even more valuable in some ways. They conjure up the mood and atmosphere of the time so vividly I felt I was living it with them.'

'I know what you mean,' she replied with feeling. 'Rose was a well-brought-up girl sheltered from the squalor and suffering she soon witnessed, but she was so determined she even lied about her age to get accepted. It's clear from her diary that she found rich rewards in helping the wounded.' She sighed. 'It makes my life seem horribly trivial.'

Ewen reached out a hand and took hers. 'Not in the least trivial, Rosanna. You're educating the next generation. And my aim is to make sure Harry and Rose's generation is never forgotten.'

'Amen to that.' Rosanna detached her hand swiftly, before he discovered her pulse was racing.

'I'm very grateful to Harry and Rose,' said Ewen, his voice deepening. 'Without them I might never have met you.'

Rosanna cast a wary glance at him.

'I felt I knew Rose already, of course,' he went on. 'But I never imagined I'd meet her in the flesh, in the person of her granddaughter.'

'I may resemble her a little, but otherwise I'm nothing like her,' warned Rosanna sharply, worried about where this was leading. 'She was very much a woman of her time. I'm totally different. I could never have been as noble as Rose. When Gerald Rivers turned up out of the blue, shell-shocked and minus an arm, Rose felt she had no option other than to marry him. So she wrote that heart-rending letter to Harry.'

'Who did his level best to get killed after receiving it. But in the usual way of things, of course, he got himself decorated instead.' Ewen shook his head. 'If this were fiction, Rose would have had his child, Gerald Rivers would have brought it up as his own and you and I, Rosanna Carey, would be related.'

His eyes locked with hers. Something molten in their depths touched a dangerous, responsive chord, and she looked away quickly, shaking her head.

'In actual fact my mother wasn't born until the thirties. Though she hardly remembers her father. He died when she was four.'

The silence which followed was so protracted, Rosanna grew restless at last and got up to break it. 'Shall we make a start?'

Ewen followed her through the sitting room into the hall. Rosanna was suddenly so burningly conscious of his physical presence in the confined space that she tripped on a rug and his hands shot out to save her, closing on her waist. He drew in a sharp, unsteady breath and turned her to face him. For a long, tense moment they stared into each other's eyes, then Ewen Fraser pulled her into his arms and kissed her.

'I've been wanting to do that from the first moment I saw you,' he muttered against her mouth, and kissed her again, his lips parting hers with such hunger she was shaken to the depths. She yielded helplessly, lost in the overpowering intimacy of the sensation as his tongue caressed hers, and he held her so tightly she could feel the powerful urgency surging through his body into hers like an electric charge. He raised his head at last, breathing unevenly, and stared down into her dazed, astonished eyes. 'Are you going to show me the door, Rosanna?' he asked hoarsely.

Appalled to find she was trembling from head to foot, she raised her chin militantly. 'Why? It was only a kiss.'

'Was it?' he said harshly.

'Yes,' she said in desperation, and broke free to precede him into the kitchen, where the bright overhead light dispersed any remnants of intimacy. Rosanna faced him, suddenly angry with herself. And with Ewen. 'I admit it's my fault as much as yours,' she said, her eyes stormy. 'I obviously misled you by letting you come here again tonight. I've got some information you want, and most of it you can have. But that's as far as it goes.'

'Then why the hell did you let me kiss you like that?' he demanded hotly.

Rosanna's face fell. 'You took me by surprise,' she muttered.

'You could have called a halt long before you did.'

'I'm aware of that.' She shrugged. 'I suppose I was a bit beglamoured by what happened to Harry and Rose. Some of it must have rubbed off. Would you have preferred a slap in the face?'

'Damn right I would,' he said bitterly, and held her chair for her. 'Right. Down to business. Let's get this over with.'

The tension lay heavy in the air between them, but they worked quickly. An hour later a pile of neatly correlated research material was stacked beside the boxes.

'Now comes the awkward bit,' said Rosanna, squaring her shoulders. 'I need a favour.'

Ewen ran a hand through his hair, eyeing her narrowly. 'What kind of favour?'

'Would you agree to an exchange?' she asked reluctantly. 'Rose's letters for Harry's? I want to try my hand at a novel. Not a serious, historical novel like yours. Just a romantic story about two star-crossed lovers in the past whose descendants get it together in the present.'

Ewen was silent for some time before he raised a daunting eyebrow. 'Have you ever had anything published?'

'No.'

'Have you ever tried your hand at fiction before?'

'No.'

'Then I wish you luck.' Ewen lounged back in his chair negligently, long legs crossed at the ankle. He shrugged. 'All right. You can keep Rose's letters. I haven't seen her diary, of course, but that's likely to be more use to you than to me, anyway, if you're concocting a romance. My focus will be on the Great War itself, following the lives of two friends, once students together in Heidelberg, now soldiers in opposing armies. Only a small section will be devoted to the doomed love affair. As a final twist the lovers are torn apart, but the friends are reunited after the war.'

Something in the pejorative way he said 'concocting a romance' needled Rosanna. 'That's fine, then,' she said tightly. 'No harm done.'

'Right.' Ewen rose to his feet. 'If you could spare some photographs of the period to go with Harry's letters, and the rest of the stuff, I'd be grateful. I'll take copies and return them, of course.'

'Of course,' said Rosanna, feeling suddenly depressed. 'Take what you want.'

He sifted through them again, chose half a dozen, then looked at a more modern photograph of Rose on the beach with her child. 'The family likeness is very marked. That's how you'll look in a few years' time.'

'Follow me,' said Rosanna abruptly, and led him across the hall to another sitting room where several silver-framed photographs were grouped together on a small table. One was her parents' wedding picture, two others were of herself and Sam in their degree robes and mortar boards. The fourth was a formal portrait of a lady with dark eyes still brilliant under her white hair, the smile familiar from Harry Manners' treasured portrait of Rose.

'Taken the year before she died,' said Rosanna huskily.

'And still beautiful.' Ewen gazed at the photograph for a long time, then turned away. 'Thank you for letting me see her.'

'It needn't make any difference to your novel,' she assured him as she saw him to the door. 'You're bound to score a big success again. Mine will be nothing like that, even if I manage to get it written, much less published. No one will ever connect yours with mine.'

Ewen shrugged. 'I doubt if we'll trespass on each other's preserves. If I do,' he added deliberately, 'you can sue me.'

'As if I would!' she said scornfully. 'Just one more thing. The portrait of Rose.'

'Sorry. I'm keeping that. You'll have to make do with Harry.'

Rosanna looked up at him in entreaty. 'But we don't have one like that, Ewen. Couldn't you take a copy of it with the others and let me have the original back?'

He looked down at her in silence for a moment. 'I'll compromise. You can have the copy. I'll keep the original. Unless,' he added, with a tigerish, explicit smile, 'you have some kind of persuasion in mind?'

Heat rose in Rosanna's face and she backed away. 'You're angry with me,' she said unsteadily. 'Why?'

His smile was unsettling as he followed her step for step as she retreated. 'Because I keep confusing you with sweet, passionate Rose, I suppose, whereas all the time cool, practical Rosanna was merely using me for her own ends.'

She opened her mouth to deny this, then thought better of it as she found herself backed up against the newel-post at the foot of the stairs. It was neither the time nor the place to confess she'd wanted to see him again for his own sake.

'I've been gazing at that portrait for weeks,' said Ewen softly, his eyes locked with hers. 'I thought I was seeing things when you opened the door to me.'

Rosanna swallowed. 'I'm not Rose, and you're not Harry.' She dodged away, but Ewen caught her easily, and locked his arms round her.

'True, Rosanna Carey,' he said huskily, 'yet it seems unbelievable that we've only just met.

I've been living with that photograph, reading Rose's letters, and then I find you, in the glowing, irresistible flesh. Rose reincarnated.'

'I'm—not—Rose,' she said through her teeth.

'Better still. You're warm flesh and blood— and alive,' he said hoarsely, and brought his mouth down hard on hers. At the touch of his lips her breath left her body and the blood pounded in her ears as Ewen Fraser knocked her defences flat for the second time. Held fast against the tall, slim body which grew tense with demand, Rosanna took a regrettably long time to come to her senses at last and tear her mouth from his. Ewen raised his head a fraction to look down into her eyes, their ragged, uneven breathing mingling as she shook her head violently.

'Why are you trembling?' he panted. 'Just as you said, it was only a kiss.'

She struggled to get free. 'Let me go. Please!'

To her fury he suddenly chuckled, shaking his head as he held her closer. In command of himself again, he was so blatantly enjoying himself she wanted to scratch his laughing, slanted eyes out.

'Oh, no!' he retorted. 'Do you think I'm a fool? I may never get the opportunity again. Don't be afraid, Rosanna. I promise I wouldn't harm Rose Norman's granddaughter for the world.'

She ground her teeth in fury. 'You won't get the chance. When I allow someone to make love to me it's because they want *me*, Rosanna Carey, not a ghost.'

'So the men you know only make love to you when you allow it?' said Ewen with interest. 'Is that satisfactory?'

'On my part yes. I don't know about theirs.' Her eyes flashed coldly. 'Besides, we're not talking in the plural. There's only one.'

Ewen leaned against the newel-post without easing his hold on her in the slightest. To break free she'd have to make a fight of it. At which point Rosanna made a mortifying discovery. She didn't want to fight. She actually enjoyed the sensation of being desired so much he wouldn't let her go. And desire her he did. In such close physical contact it was a fact impossible to ignore.

'I thought there must be,' he said, sighing theatrically. 'Who's the lucky man? And where is he? Am I likely to see him hurtling through the door at any minute to wrest you from my arms?'

Rosanna would have given a lot to say yes. 'No,' she muttered into his shirt-front. 'He's a doctor, gaining experience in the States to add BTA to his qualifications.'

'BTA?'

'Been to America.'

Ewen grinned, and raised her face to his. 'Would he mind if he knew you were here like this? With me?'

'He'd better,' she snapped.

'Then I might as well give him something to mind about.' Ewen stifled her protest with an engulfing kiss, parting her lips with his marauding tongue. He made no move to caress her with his hands, but went on kissing her with unflagging relish, his arms locking her so close against him, their hearts thumped in unison. Rosanna had never been kissed like this, by someone taking so much pleasure in the process that the kisses in themselves were more erotic than anything experienced before. Even in the arms of Dr David Norton.

The thought struck Rosanna like a thunderbolt, and she wrenched herself away, clutching the newel-post. Ewen's arms dropped and he stood back, his eyes slitted in his taut face, their uneven breathing the only sound to break the silence.

'Time I went,' he said gruffly at last.

'Yes.' She took in a deep, shaky breath.

But neither made any move. Rosanna knew she should speed Ewen Fraser on his way, in case he took her silence for acquiescence, some kind of tacit invitation to stay and take up where he had just left off. Which, she realised, was exactly what she wanted, deep down. Which was incredible. Even if there were no David she just wasn't the type to fling herself into the arms of a man she'd known for one solitary day. Especially one who couldn't separate Rosanna Carey of now from Rose Norman of then. If she were ever mad enough to let Ewen Fraser make love to her she would never be sure if he wanted her for herself or because she was the incarnation of Rose.

Rosanna pulled herself together and released her death grip on the newel-post. 'Right,' she said, in a voice intended to be brisk, but which came out so unlike her own she hardly recognised it. She cleared her throat and tried again, wishing Ewen would move, instead of looking at her as though committing her face to memory. 'Goodnight, then, Ewen. Good luck with the book.'

'And you,' he said quietly. He turned to pick up his briefcase. 'Goodnight, Rosanna. Thank you for the drink. I'll return everything in due course.' He reached into a pocket for his wallet and took out a card. 'Here's my number should you need to contact me.'

'Thank you.' Rosanna took it from him, privately vowing to have nothing at all to do with him again. Ever. 'Ewen,' she said impulsively as he went out, and he turned sharply in the porch.

'Yes?'

'I had the idea of writing about Rose before I'd even met you, or knew what you wanted.

And I'm not using information that belongs to you, except for his photograph, and you can have that back if you want.'

'I already have one very like it. You keep Harry. I'll keep my beautiful Rose.' He smiled crookedly, and she shook her dishevelled head.

'You're in love with a ghost, Ewen Fraser.'

His eyes glittered under the porch light. 'If you mean that what happened between us just now is likely to haunt me, you're right. But there's no ghost involved, just the memory of you in my arms. *You*, Rosanna. Goodnight.'

CHAPTER THREE

Rosanna rang her parents next morning, gave her mother a brief account of the meeting with Ewen Fraser, and told her Harry's letters had been duly handed over.

'He gave me Rose's letters in return.'

'How wonderful,' said Henrietta Carey, the catch in her voice plainly audible down the line. 'I can't wait to read them. What did you think of Harry and his letters?'

'Quite a man. Poor Rose. Poor Harry, too. Apparently he never married.'

'How sad. Did you like Ewen Fraser, by the way?'

'Yes,' said Rosanna with perfect truth. 'He's—rather charming.'

'Are you going to see him again?'

'No, Mother.'

'Have you heard from David lately?''

'Yes, of course. He rang on Sunday, as usual. He's working very hard.'

'I'm sure he is, darling. Sam sends his love, by the way.'

'Is he well?'

'Fighting fit. He told you to come with us next time.'

After talking to her parents the house seemed empty to Rosanna. She'd slept very badly after Ewen's departure the night before, burning with guilt over the disloyalty to David. But it was only a *kiss*, she told herself. David would understand. Not that she was going to tell him, just in case he didn't. News like that didn't travel well.

In spite of her restless night she'd been awake at first light, and the day stretched emptily in front of her. Which was what she'd longed for last week when she was working like a dog for Charlie, she reminded herself irritably, so she'd better make the most of it, and start on some serious research for her novel.

A visit to the local library provided her with a stack of helpful literature, fact and fiction, including Siegfried Sassoon's account of life in the trenches. And on the way home Rosanna called into a bookshop and bought a copy of *Savage Dawn*. Just out of curiosity.

From now on, thought Rosanna dryly, she could hardly complain about having nothing to do.

She resisted the temptation to read Ewen's book first. Instead she went out into the garden with a picnic lunch and started on Sassoon's memoirs to get herself in the mood.

Rosanna read all afternoon and evening, regularly dipping into the factual, pictorial accounts alongside Sassoon's graphic, understated account of trench warfare. She ate her supper while she read, and made notes and drank endless mugs of tea and coffee. By eight in the evening her eyes were protesting and she was so stiff from sitting in one position she had a long, leisurely soak in the bath, watched television for an hour or so, then locked up and went to bed with Ewen's book.

His style was spare, but so evocative. The African heat fairly sizzled from the pages as she read. Rosanna was drawn to the soldier hero from the first, and found herself identifying with the woman he loved to such a degree that her heart began hammering during the first love scene between them. Afterwards she lay awake in the dark for hours, shaken by the fact that Ewen's written word conjured up his own lovemaking all too vividly. She burned with guilt, furious with herself for responding so helplessly. She was going to marry David Norton. She'd known David for ever, and his lovemaking was very... Very what? Rosanna let out a deep, irritated sigh. At the moment she couldn't remember what it was like. Whereas she could feel Ewen Fraser's kisses on her mouth even now.

Next morning Rosanna was up early again, in need of exercise before any more reading. To her surprise she found two letters addressed to her amongst her parents' mail. One, as expected, was from David, but the writing on the other envelope was unfamiliar. She made herself read every word of David's cheery, affectionate missive before she opened the other letter, her heart skipping a beat when she saw Ewen's signature. He began rather formally by thanking her for his uncle's letters, and the evenings Rosanna had given up to help him with his research. Then he went on to say how grateful he was to Harry Manners for leading him to a meeting with Rose Norman's granddaughter.

In another way I regret it. Deeply. You were right. I am haunted. But not by Rose Norman. I can't sleep for thoughts of *you*, Rosanna. I keep seeing your face, feeling your lips parting under mine, the warmth of your delectable body in my arms.

He went on in the same vein for several more lines, then signed himself simply as 'Ewen'. Rosanna stared blindly at the black, slanted script of what could only be described as a love letter. Lust, not *love*, she told herself scornfully. Ewen Fraser had merely taught her a chemistry lesson, amazing her by her response to a virtual stranger. And for no particular reason that she could fathom. Ewen was no macho he-man bursting with testosterone. Nevertheless there was something lethally attractive about his tall, loose-limbed body, and the wide, expressive mouth that knew so well how to kiss a girl senseless... She took a deep breath, made herself some coffee, then went out for a run in the park to burn off feelings roused by a few words on paper. Clever devil, she thought bitterly. No wonder his books sold.

Next morning Rosanna received a second letter from Ewen, telling her how he was getting on with his book and asking about the progress of hers. And once more he ended with a few pulse-quickening lines which left her shaken and restless, and in need of a longer run than usual before she could settle to her research. Afterwards she went round to the Claytons' house and used Charlie's machine to send Ewen a fax, telling him to stop writing to her. And to her surprise, and utterly savage disappointment, he did.

On Saturday, a week later, Rosanna went round to the flat in Bayswater to collect some clothes, and found Louise on her way out to spend the weekend with a new man. This was definitely the one, said Louise, starry-eyed, but Rosanna had heard that one before. Often. She laughed affectionately, wished Louise good luck, then went off to do some solitary window-shopping. After a visit to the cinema later on Rosanna finally went home, feeling thoroughly out of sorts. There had been no more letters from Ewen, and none from David, either. He rang her instead, to apologise for lack of time to write, and promised to come home for a holiday soon. And, to make matters worse, she missed Ewen's brief, passionate notes far more than she missed David's accounts of life in Boston.

On impulse Rosanna rang David's Boston number, but a recorded message was her only reward. She left a brief greeting and rang off, feeling restless and lonely, resigned to a Saturday evening with only the television and a novel for company.

When the phone rang later she was in the kitchen, trying to whip up the enthusiasm to make herself something to eat. She brightened, and raced into the hall to answer it. 'Hi, David!'

'Sorry to disappoint you, Rosanna,' said a deep, husky voice very different from David Norton's. But just as recognisable.

'Who is this?' she said, after a pause.

His laugh raised the hairs down her spine. 'Ewen. As you well know.'

'Hello, Ewen. This is a surprise. How are you?'

'All the better for talking to you, Rosanna. Though I didn't expect to at this time on a Saturday night.'

'Why not?'

'I was sure you'd be out, socialising some- where.'

'Louise is otherwise engaged.'

'And is she the only one you go out with?'

'No. I have another friend, Maxine, but she's on holiday.'

'You mean that while the good doctor's in the States you do without male company of any kind?'

'Not necessarily. Sometimes I see old col- lege friends. But no one's around at the mo- ment.'

'In that case would he object if you had din- ner with me?'

'I have no idea. Besides, it's me you should be asking, not David.'

'I am asking you, Rosanna. Will you?'

Rosanna wanted very badly to say yes. 'I don't think that's a good idea,' she said at last.

'Why not?'

'You can ask that, after the letters you sent me?'

'Were they so offensive?'

She was silent for a moment. 'Not offensive, exactly. But you shouldn't have written to me like that.'

'I haven't since you told me to stop.'

'I know. Thank you.'

'Something's wrong, Rosanna,' he persisted. 'Tell me.'

'You'll laugh,' she said, depressed.

'From your tone it doesn't seem likely!' He paused. 'Rosanna, all I'm asking is an evening spent together. My intentions are of the best. Or are you convinced my sole object is seduction?'

'I hope I'm not so conceited,' she retorted. 'Why do you want to see me?'

'I can tell something's wrong. I want to know what it is.'

Rosanna sighed dispiritedly. 'It's nothing you can do anything about.'

'Rosanna,' said Ewen after a pause, 'is it something to do with David?'

'No. Nothing at all.'

'I see. Or rather I don't see.' He paused. 'Let's discuss it over dinner. Though if you don't want to talk about it I won't press you. Afterwards I'll deliver you to your door without even a peck on the cheek.'

Why not? she thought defiantly, avoiding her eyes in the mirror. She couldn't stay home *all* the time. 'Then thank you, I'll come. It's very kind of you.'

'Not really. It's the journalist in me, scenting a story.'

Ewen rang back later to confirm dinner at a favourite restaurant of his in Shepherd's Bush, as long as they didn't mind eating late. Rosanna, who hadn't intended eating very much at all, assured him she didn't mind a bit, but told him not to come for her. She would meet him at the restaurant around nine.

Which, she thought, running upstairs, gave her a couple of hours to make herself look as contemporary as possible. Her spirits high, Rosanna put on the sleeveless, low-cut black dress she kept for special occasions, added sheer black stockings, strappy black suede shoes, and took a long time over her face. She brushed her waving dark hair back as severely as possible, and secured it at the nape of her neck with a tortoiseshell clasp, then, with a touch of defiance, pinned the gold rose to the shoulder of her dress. The result, she thought, satisfied, was a far cry from young Rose Norman.

Ewen was waiting when she arrived at the restaurant. He wore a fawn linen suit and his face looked tired under the thick black hair, dark smudges of fatigue under his eyes. But when he caught sight of her the eyes lit up, and Rosanna's heart gave a sudden, unsettling thump as he came towards her, hand out-stretched.

'Rosanna, you look ravishing!' He seated her in a corner of the crowded bar, his eyes moving over her with unconcealed pleasure. 'That's the famous rose, of course, but other-wise thoroughly modern Rosanna,' he said with a grin, and she smiled back wryly. He really was a clever devil.

'Just so there's no confusion,' she said lightly, and agreed to champagne when he told her he was celebrating the racing start he'd made on his book.

'How about you?' he asked.

'I'm very well,' she assured him.

'I can see that.' The look in his eyes brought such heat to her face, Rosanna gave fervent, secret thanks for the naturally matt complexion which disguised it. 'What shall we drink to?' he asked, filling her glass.

'Rose and Harry,' she said promptly.

'Amen to that.' Ewen drank some of his wine, then turned his attention to the menu. 'Let's choose, then we'll be free to discuss this problem of yours.'

Rosanna was sorry now she'd ever admitted to having a problem. But if she hadn't, she reminded herself, she wouldn't be here with Ewen now. Where she was dangerously happy to be. The entire occasion was bringing light to a week which had felt like a dark tunnel of disappointment and frustration.

'Could we leave my problem until after dinner, please?' she said ruefully. 'I'd like to enjoy the meal first. Tell me about your novel instead.'

Ewen's eyes narrowed searchingly, but he made no move to press her. 'As I told you, I started the research for it as soon as I finished *Savage Dawn*, and I'd already mapped out the story between the two friends. Then I read about Harry's meeting with Rose and the love theme just fell into place.'

'I'll look forward to reading it.' She smiled a little. '*Savage Dawn* was brilliant, by the way. I couldn't put it down.'

His eyebrows rose. 'You mean you actually bought it?'

'Yes.'

'Rosanna, I would have given you a copy if I'd thought you were interested.' His smile was wry. 'I tend not to force my efforts on the unwilling.'

'I didn't like to ask.'

His eyes gleamed suddenly. 'Afraid I might expect something in return?'

'Certainly not,' she said loftily. 'Just *afraid* you were still angry because I wanted to write on the same subject.'

He shrugged. 'I admit I wasn't too pleased at the time. I thought you let me see you again because you liked my company, not just to wheedle Rose's letters away from me. My ego took a beating.'

'You came to see me for the same reason, where Harry was concerned.'

'Not the second time, as you know perfectly well,' he said, so quietly she barely heard him above the conversations going on around them. But the gleam in his eyes made his meaning unmistakable.

'Let's talk about something else,' she said hastily, looking away. 'Have you been watching the new Jane Austen serial?'

'I haven't watched anything since I started the book. While the muse is with me I work until I can't see straight, then microwave something vaguely edible, go to bed and fall asleep listening to the radio.'

Rosanna frowned in disapproval. 'That can't be good for your health. Or your social life.'

He shrugged. 'The latter's non-existent when I'm writing.'

'I find it hard to believe that,' she retorted. 'Your social life is so well documented I recognised you almost at once. You've been photographed often enough with various beautiful ladies, Ewen Fraser.'

He looked at her very squarely. 'But rarely with the same one, Rosanna. Lately, anyway. Most of it was just publicity. My lifestyle tends to put paid to lasting relationships. When I was a full-time journalist it was the long hours and my habit of turning up late for evenings out, or sometimes not at all. Now it's even worse. The most recent lady in my life gave up on me rather than play second fiddle to my computer.'

'Was she right about that?' asked Rosanna curiously.

'In a way. She wanted marriage, I didn't, so we split up. Marriage doesn't appeal, I'm afraid.' He raised an eyebrow. 'What are your views on the subject?'

'Very dull and conventional.' She smiled. 'I'm the original old-fashioned girl. It's always been marriage for David and me.'

'Everyone to their own taste,' he said lightly as the waiter approached. 'Good, our meal is ready. I'm hungry.'

Ewen made no attempt to press Rosanna about her problem over the meal, which they ate in a secluded little booth at the back of the restaurant, sharing the same bench seat. Which, she thought, had its disadvantages. The meal was delicious, but sitting so close to Ewen made it very difficult to concentrate on the food. She'd expected to face him across a table. Instead they were enclosed in unexpected intimacy, cut off from the rest of the room by a concealing array of potted greenery. And every time his arm brushed hers, or his foot came into contact with her own under the table, she felt such a surge of electricity it was difficult not to show it.

When the coffee arrived after the meal Ewen moved closer, half turned towards her, the dark rings under his eyes less pronounced now.

'Aren't you going to praise me for my forbearance?'

'For not asking what's wrong?' Rosanna nodded, smiling wryly. 'Particularly as you'd probably rather be tapping away at your keyboard than trying to cheer me up.'

'Are you mad? Of course I wouldn't. What man would?' he said with emphasis, then grinned. 'And to be honest it was a change to eat a proper meal for once.'

'You certainly look better for it,' she said reprovingly. 'You shouldn't resort to a microwave all the time. It doesn't take long to throw a cold meal together.'

'You sound like my mother,' he said resignedly, then smiled crookedly. 'But you don't look like her.'

'You mean I look like Rose!'

'Actually you don't tonight. You look so alluring it's very bad for me.' He slid closer still and took her hand in his, looking into her eyes. 'Strange as it may seem—no matter what you've read about me—it's not my habit to socialise with women already spoken for,

Rosanna Carey. Talking of which, have you heard from young Dr Kildare lately?'

'Of course I have.'

'When's he coming home to see you?'

'As soon as he can,' she said defensively. 'He's very busy.'

'He's also a fool,' said Ewen flatly.

'How can you say that?' she retorted. 'You don't know him.'

'I know *you*, Rosanna. And if the man's not worried about leaving a woman like you alone for months on end—' He raised his free hand. 'I rest my case.'

'I suppose that's a compliment.'

'It was intended as one.'

'Then thank you.' Rosanna hesitated, then gave in to temptation. 'Are you very tired, Ewen?'

His eyes narrowed. 'Why?'

'Would you mind coming back with me to the house? There's something I want to give you.'

'I'd be delighted, as you know very well.' He smiled into her eyes, his fingers tightening. 'I intended to see you safely home anyway,

Rosanna. Am I allowed to ask what I'm about to receive? Will I be truly thankful for it?'

'I hope so,' she said lightly. She detached her hand very deliberately and got to her feet. 'If not I'll keep it.'

'I'll treasure whatever you give me,' he assured her. 'Would you like a nightcap while we wait for a cab?'

'No, thanks, not after champagne.' She smiled at him. 'Thank you for the meal.'

'My pleasure, Rosanna. Not that you ate much of it,' he added, and turned away to pay the bill, and a few minutes later they were in a taxi on their way back to Ealing. And rather to Rosanna's surprise Ewen made no move to touch her on the journey home, but sat, circumspect, in his own half of the seat.

Rosanna saw the red light blinking on the phone the minute she unlocked the door. 'Go into the sitting room,' she told Ewen. 'I'll make coffee. Would you like some brandy with it?'

'No, thanks.' Ewen nodded towards the machine. 'Aren't you going to play that back? It might be urgent.'

He leaned against the newel-post, eyeing her with challenge, but she went past him into the kitchen to fill the kettle, then returned without haste to press the button.

'Hi, Rosanna,' said David's familiar voice. 'Got your message. Catch you later.'

'The missing lover, I assume,' said Ewen with irony.

'That was David, yes,' she returned. 'Do go in and sit down. I shan't be long.'

But Ewen followed her back to the kitchen. 'He sounds rather transatlantic. Has he been out there long?'

'Six months.'

'And he hasn't been back since?'

'No.' Rosanna poured boiling water on instant coffee, and handed him a beaker. 'Black, no sugar.'

'You remembered. Thank you. Why hasn't he been home?' he added persistently.

'He was all set to come, twice, but something came up at the last minute each time.' Rosanna added milk to her coffee, went into the sitting room, and curled up on a corner of the sofa. 'I hope to fly out to him for a break before I start work.'

Ewen followed and sat down beside her. 'Enough of the doctor, then. Let's talk about this problem of yours.'

'It's a decision more than a problem.' She touched a hand to the rosewood box on the table beside her. 'I'm letting you have Rose's diary and letters. Though naturally we'd like them back when you finish the book.'

He frowned, surprised. 'Why the change of heart, Rosanna?'

She gave him a rueful little smile. 'It's quite simple, Ewen. When it came to writing a novel I thoroughly enjoyed the research part. But actually creating a piece of fiction is beyond me. I tried hard, but I just can't do it.'

CHAPTER FOUR

EWEN looked at her in silence, then took her hand. 'Are you sure, Rosanna? Would you like me to read some of it?'

'No!' She shuddered. 'Much too embarrassing.'

'Maybe you're too self-critical.'

'I doubt it!' Rosanna paused, frowning. 'On the other hand, perhaps your opinion would be a good thing. As long as you're honest.'

'I will be. How much have you written?'

'One chapter. Over and over again. Revised until I can't even tell if it makes sense. Do you want to read it now?' she added awkwardly.

'No. I'll take it home with me. My eyes would go on strike if I tried reading anything tonight.' His eyes gleamed. 'Besides, it gives me the perfect excuse for seeing you again.'

'It needn't,' she retorted. 'You could always post it back to me.'

'Then it's no deal,' he said, grinning. 'When do you want the verdict?'

'I'm in no rush,' she assured him wryly.

'Let's make it tomorrow,' he said with decision. 'I fancy a day off. Come round to my place for tea. Or dinner.'

'All from the microwave?'

'O ye of little faith!'

She thought it over. Sunday yawned emptily in front of her now she'd given up all hope of trying to write her novel. 'Tea sounds respectable. I'll settle for that.'

'Good.' He smiled, and released her hand. 'And now, Miss Carey, I shall ring for a cab, and take myself off.'

Afterwards, in the hall, Ewen put her manuscript in the rosewood box, eyeing her searchingly. 'Are you sure about this?'

'Certain,' she said, depressed. 'When you've read my little effort you'll know why.'

He bent suddenly and kissed her cheek. 'A second opinion may be different.' He reached out a hand to touch the place he'd kissed and Rosanna stood very still, not daring to move. She saw his eyes narrow to a familiar gold glitter and felt her pulse race in response. Then the phone rang.

She turned her back on Ewen and lifted the receiver with an unsteady hand.

'Hi, Rosanna,' said David. 'I've got you this time. I tried the flat but someone called Paula said you were still in Ealing. Where've you been? Out with a new lover?'

'Where else?' said Rosanna breathlessly, burningly aware of the man standing close behind her.

David laughed indulgently and went on to tell her about a recent crisis in the busy Boston hospital, but Rosanna lost the thread of his tale as Ewen put the box down very deliberately on the hall table, his eyes holding hers in the mirror. He bent suddenly to kiss the nape of her neck and she stifled a gasp.

'So what do you think?' asked David.

Rosanna stared at the phone wildly. 'Sorry,' she said hoarsely. 'The line's bad this end. I didn't catch that.' Tremors ran through her as Ewen kissed the hollow behind each ear, and she clenched her teeth to stop them chattering.

'Have you got a cold?' demanded David.

'No,' she said with difficulty. 'Tell me what you said.'

David told her he'd been asked to stay on longer than originally planned. 'Good experience, Rosanna,' he added apologetically. 'Seems a shame to pass it up.'

'Then don't,' she advised him shortly.

'Are you sure you're OK? You sound really weird.'

'I'm a long way away,' she reminded him, staring into the mirror, mesmerised, as slanted, glittering eyes held hers in a look which made her heart thump.

Then the doorbell rang. Ewen whispered, 'Four tomorrow,' to her reflection, collected the box and let himself out.

'What was that?' demanded David.

'A taxi. A friend came to keep me company. You remember Maxine?' said Rosanna in a guilty rush.

'Not a new lover, then,' teased David.

She thrust a strand of hair into place, glad he couldn't see her face. 'It's great they want to keep you for a bit,' she said quickly. 'Can't you come home first?'

'Not for a while. Soon, though.'

'I could come out to you,' she suggested.

There was a pause. 'Great idea, Rosie. We'll fix a date.'

'Right. I'll look forward to it. Don't work too hard.'

'I won't. I even went fishing last weekend. Great fun. You'd have loved it.'

Rosanna doubted it. Fishing was one of David's interests she'd known from the first she'd never share. 'I'm glad you had a good time.'

'Rosie, are you sure you're all right? Not coming down with something?'

'I'm fine,' she assured him.

'If you say so. I'll ring again soon, once I've sorted something out.'

'You do that. Goodnight, David.'

Rosanna was in bed when the phone rang again. With a sigh she slid out of bed and went into her parents' room. David again, probably, wanting to know if she had a temperature.

'Did I get you out of bed?' asked Ewen.

Heat rushed to Rosanna's face. 'Yes.'

'I felt I should apologise for sabotaging your conversation with the doctor.'

'You didn't.'

'So you had a long talk once I'd gone.'

'Yes.'

'Is he coming home soon?'

'No.'

'When he does are you getting married?'

'Not for a while, no. We both need some career-building first.'

'Very clinical.'

'Very sensible!'

'I could describe my response to you with a hundred different words, Rosanna. "Sensible", as must have been painfully obvious earlier on, isn't one of them.'

Rosanna smiled involuntarily. 'I wanted to kick you in the shin.'

'Why didn't you?'

'You might have howled loud enough for David to hear.'

'True. How did you explain the doorbell?'

'I said a taxi had come for a friend.'

'Ah. Did he buy that?'

'Yes.'

'But you didn't tell him I was the friend.'

'No.'

There was a pause. 'Rosanna, tomorrow I promise to behave like a perfect gent. Scout's honour.'

'Can I have that in writing?'

'Is that a yes?' he said swiftly. 'Will you still come?'

Out of pride she kept him waiting a moment or two longer, but in the end she ignored her conscience and said yes as he wanted.

'What a sparing lady you are with words, Miss Carey.'

'You obviously haven't read my little piece!'

'No. I'll do that in the morning. Tonight I just wanted to make sure you hadn't changed your mind about tomorrow.'

'Why?'

'You know why, Rosanna. Goodnight.'

Next morning Rosanna had a chat with her parents, then eyed the clothes in her wardrobe, frowning. Why, she thought suddenly, was it always so imperative to look her best when she

saw Ewen Fraser? Last night it had been relatively easy, the inevitable little black dress.
But today it was hot, with June sunshine blaz-
ing down on the capital, and without collecting
something from the flat the only thing suitable—and unseen before by Ewen Fraser—was
a long, fluted skirt in dark blue cotton printed
with faded cream roses. Very appropriate, she
thought wryly, and added a plain navy T-shirt
as an antidote to too much romanticism.

That Ewen approved was obvious by the
gleam in his eyes when he opened the door of
his smart little mews house to her later that
afternoon.

'Beautiful *and* punctual,' he said, opening
the door wide for her. 'An unbeatable combi-
nation. Welcome, Rosanna.'

'Thank you.' She looked round with interest. 'So this is your house. I like it very much.
it's so—'

'Empty?' He grinned, and waved a hand
around him. 'All my own taste.'

Spiral stairs bisected the living area. In one
half a low circular table stood on a worn
Persian rug between a pair of sofas covered in

natural linen. The other section was emptier still, furnished with only a pair of deep leather chairs and a television, every available inch of wall space lined with crowded bookshelves.

'Uncluttered,' said Rosanna approvingly. 'Very nice indeed.'

'I haven't been here long. This is as far as I've got.' He nodded his head towards a door at the back of the room. 'The kitchen—alias the room with the microwave—is out there. Would you like tea now?'

'Not just yet.' Rosanna sat down on one of the sofas. 'Break it to me first. Did you read my manuscript?'

Ewen sat down opposite her. 'I did,' he said gently. 'And it wasn't as dire as you made out.'

'But it wasn't good either, was it?' she said gloomily.

'Not if you're aiming for something romantic. It's well written, but it lacked emotional intensity. It's more like an essay than a story.'

'I know. Sad, isn't it? Thank you for the kind words, anyway.' She sighed. 'At the end

I felt I'd written the wretched thing in my life-blood. Fiction obviously isn't for me.'

Ewen leaned forward, his hands clasped between his knees. 'Maybe not. Though don't rule out a further shot at it in the future. In the meantime you could put your talents to other use this summer, Rosanna. If you'd like to.'

She eyed him warily. 'Doing what exactly?'

'Even from this one chapter I can see you did your homework thoroughly.'

'Thank you. As I said before, the research part was no problem at all.'

'In that case how do you feel about helping me out with mine?'

Rosanna looked into the intent hazel eyes in surprise. 'But I thought you'd already done that.'

'I have. But when I'm writing I still verify at every stage.' He leaned nearer. 'If I printed each chapter as I go along, just getting the story down in full flow, as I'd prefer to, you could read the drafts, tidy them up and check the references, and when I need more information, as I invariably do, you could save me a lot of time by hunting it down for me.'

She thought about it for a moment or two. 'Does that mean you'd want me to work here?' she asked.

'Would that be a problem?'

'I suppose not.' She looked at him warily. 'But you work long hours, Ewen.'

'I wouldn't expect you to do the same,' he said quickly. 'You can keep to office hours, or any hours you want. Any time you spare me will lighten my load. My deadline's looming, and I'm already a bit pushed. Naturally I would pay you,' he added.

Rosanna frowned indignantly. 'I wasn't thinking about money!'

Ewen jumped to his feet. 'I know you weren't. Just sit and think about it for a bit while I organise tea.'

'Do you want any help?'

'I remember you objected to that kind of thing in your last job,' he said, grinning. 'You just mull over my suggestion while I'm out there making scones and so on.'

'Making *scones*?' she said, laughing.

He went off to the kitchen, leaving Rosanna deep in thought. And very tempted to take him up on his offer. He was right. She had loved the research part of the writing. But she doubted the wisdom of working at such close quarters with Ewen Fraser. There was a strong element of risk in the secret pleasure she took in his company. *And* in the very open pleasure he took in hers.

Ewen came in with a large tea tray and put it down on the table in front of Rosanna. 'I was joking about the scones, but I did make toast. The walnut cake was donated by my mother, I had sandwiches ready and there's some anchovy spread for the toast. I'm rather partial to anchovies. Will you pour, Miss Carey?'

Rosanna eyed the laden tray in astonishment. 'Goodness, Mr Fraser. I'm impressed. How do you take your tea?'

'Like my coffee.' He sat down, smiling at her. 'My brainwave of afternoon tea was inspired. Seduction and cucumber sandwiches just don't mix.'

Rosanna giggled. 'True. What does it mix with?'

Ewen took a sandwich and bit into it, then gave her a very straight look. 'I've never actually set out to seduce anyone, so I can't say.'

Between them they made short work of most of the food on the tray, and afterwards Ewen took it out to the kitchen and left it there, flatly refusing Rosanna's help. When he came back he sat down beside her with an air of purpose. 'Before you decide about my suggestion there's something I want to say.'

She eyed him apprehensively. 'That sounds ominous.'

'Not really. I'd like to make it clear that if you don't want to work for me I'll understand.' He stared down at the exquisite, faded design on the carpet.

'Understand what?' she said cautiously.

'The reason. My behaviour last night. Listening in on a private conversation. And so on.'

'Why did you listen—and so on?'

Ewen turned his head and looked her in the eye. 'Jealousy. Envy. Sheer bloody-mindedness. Take your pick.'

She looked away quickly. 'I'd like to work with you—'

'But!' he put in, resigned.

'It would have to be on a purely professional basis.'

His face cleared. 'Of course. If I promise to remember your attachment to the absent doctor, blast his eyes, is the answer yes?'

'Yes, it is,' she said simply, and Ewen gave her a smile of pure triumph.

'When could you start?'

'Tomorrow, if you like.'

'Of course I like,' he said with emphasis, then looked thoughtful. 'You know, if I installed another computer, you could read my output straight off the floppy disks. Would you print it, too? That would really speed up the process.'

Rosanna agreed with enthusiasm, and followed Ewen upstairs to inspect his study. The room was very small, with just enough space for a large desk laden with computer, printer and fax machine. The walls were lined with overflowing bookshelves, and more books lay in piles behind the desk.

'If you get another computer where would you put it?' she asked blankly.

'Downstairs by the television. I should be able to arrange it by Tuesday, I think. In the meantime,' said Ewen with mounting enthusiasm, 'perhaps you could do a little preliminary swotting.'

Rosanna bent to look through some of the books. 'I've read some of these already— Sassoon and Remarque and so on. But if you like I'll take others home to read until you're ready for me.'

'I'd rather you did the reading here, Rosanna.'

'All right. I'll come over in the morning.'

He held out his hand to help her up. 'Do you have to hurry home yet?'

'Not really. Why? Did you want me to make a start right now?'

'Of course I don't. Stay and have supper with me.' Ewen smiled, and released her hand. 'From tomorrow we'll keep everything strictly business. But tonight let's just be—friends.'

Rosanna looked at him in silence for a moment or two. She was making a habit of saying yes to Ewen Fraser, she thought wryly. In company with quite a few other women. Which was a point to remember. But the alternative was an evening alone in the big, empty house in Ealing, or a call on a friend on the off chance of finding one in. 'All right. Thank you,' she said at last. 'Are you sending out, or do I have to cook it?'

'Neither.' Ewen smiled smugly. 'I did some shopping, just in case. As someone once told me, it's not much trouble to put a cold meal together.'

Rosanna couldn't help feeling flattered that Ewen so obviously desired her company. She was well aware that he desired more than that. But some instinct assured her that now she'd made herself clear where David was concerned Ewen Fraser was a civilised man who would keep to the rules. If she wanted him to. Which she did. Of course she did.

'But I must get home early tonight,' she warned as they went downstairs. 'I'm starting a new job tomorrow, remember.'

'Talking of which,' he said briskly, 'we need to discuss money.'

'Must we?'

'Yes. How much did Clayton pay you?'

When Rosanna told him the hourly rate Ewen promptly doubled it.

'But I can't take that much,' she objected.

'Believe me, you'll earn it,' he assured her. 'And don't worry, I get my sandwich lunch delivered when I'm working, my cleaner comes in twice a week, and a laundry service deals with the shirts.'

Rosanna smiled at him, her eyes dancing. 'In that case I'll make as much coffee as you like.'

They sat down opposite each other on the sofas, Ewen leaning forward, animation in every line of him as he outlined what he'd written already, and how the plot was intended to develop.

'Of course it doesn't always go to plan. Unexpected twists happen along the way. Characters acquire a personality all their own, do things that surprise me.'

Rosanna listened, fascinated, to the deep-toned voice with the attractive, husky break in it. Ewen's enthusiasm for his work was infectious.

'I envy you the talent to produce something like this. It sounds wonderful,' she said after a while. 'I'm flattered you want me to help with the process. What happens if it doesn't work?'

He frowned. 'The plot?'

'No. Having me around. You may find my presence intrusive.'

Ewen shook his head firmly. 'I admit I couldn't share a room. But just having you on hand will be an enormous help.' He smiled a little. 'Even an inspiration in certain sections.'

'Because I look like Rose?' she said resignedly.

He shook his head. 'Because you're Rosanna. And in my eyes, as you well know, utterly desirable.'

Her heart beat thickly as their eyes locked across the small space, but Ewen raised his hands in a gesture she knew very well meant that he had no intention of acting on his words.

'I promise never to refer to it once we start work,' he assured her matter-of-factly, and jumped to his feet. 'Right. If you're determined to leave early I'd better get on with sup-per.'

'I'll help—'

'No way! That's not in the agreement.'

'It doesn't start until tomorrow, Ewen.' She followed him into the small, streamlined kitchen. 'I can't just sit and do nothing. In fact, if it's a cold meal I'm quite good at salads. Show me what there is to work with.'

Ewen gave in with open relief. 'Bossy woman.'

'You'll be glad of it tomorrow!'

'I'm glad of it tonight,' he assured her, and opened the refrigerator with a flourish. Rosanna nodded in approval as she took out two poached salmon fillets, then, after a search, added salad greens, bacon and a couple of eggs.

'Any other vegetables?'

A cupboard yielded small new potatoes, pale young carrots complete with their feathery leaves, and the shiny green pods of newly picked broad beans.

Rosanna's eyes lit up. 'Wow. Where do you buy vegetables like these?'

'Actually they were a gift.'

'Lucky old you.' Rosanna chose some beans and told him to start podding. 'Can I have a rummage through your store cupboard?'

'Help yourself! I thought you didn't like cooking.'

'This isn't cooking, more like assembling.' Rosanna pounced in triumph on a tin of anchovies and a jar of expensive olive oil, then filled two pans with water to boil.

Ewen passed the beans over, watching her activities with interest. 'Am I allowed to ask what we're having?'

'A sort of salad with a difference,' she said, and lowered eggs into one pan before tossing the beans into the other.

'Sounds good. I'll cut some bread.

Rosanna took a lemon from a bowl of fruit on the counter, and whisked the juice with the oil, then began grilling slices of bacon. When they were crisp she chopped them into the drained, cooked beans, tossed them in the dressing, added quartered hard-boiled eggs and laid the anchovies in strips on top, then arranged the salmon fillets on a bed of salad greens. 'A bit fish-orientated,' she said doubt-fully. 'I hope it's your kind of thing.'

'Perfection,' said Ewen reverently a few minutes later, after the first mouthful. 'If I paid you extra could you come up with something like this every day?'

'Not a chance,' she said, buttering a thick slice of olive bread. 'My culinary bursts of genius are few and far between.'

'So what do you live on in this flat of yours?'

'Louise, my flatmate, is quite a star in the kitchen. When her social life allows, that is. When it's my turn it's usually pasta or salad.'

'When the good doctor's in the UK,' said Ewen, his eyes on his plate, 'does he live in this flat of yours?'

'No.'

'Have you ever lived together?'

Rosanna shook her head. 'Though I've known David for years. He was at school with my brother.'

Ewen's eyebrows rose. 'Surely he's not the only man you've ever had in your life?'

'In that particular way, yes. We went to different universities and we've both had other friends, male and female.' Rosanna looked at him steadily. 'David's choice of profession means he'll take a while to realise his ambitions. But it's always been understood that when he's passed various exams and managed to get himself published a few times we'll get married.'

'I thought doctors always married nurses, or other doctors,' he said lightly.

'This one's going to marry *me*.'

CHAPTER FIVE

Ewen finished his meal in thoughtful silence, and cut himself more bread to mop up the last of the juices on his plate.

'Your doctor must be a very patient man,' he observed after a while. 'Isn't he worried that a more impetuous guy might come along and sweep you off your feet?'

'One must be willing to be swept,' she pointed out, and pushed her plate away.

'And you've never been tempted?'

Not until now, thought Rosanna with a sudden pang. 'No,' she fibbed. 'Never.'

'But are you never impatient to get married or at least set up house together and share your lives?' he went on persistently.

'I can tell you're a journalist—you never give up,' she retorted. 'And no. I'm not impatient. I've got a career of my own, remember. David and I have been together since we were teenagers. It's a way of life for us.'

Ewen slid to his feet and lifted her down from the stool, then stood with his hands at either side of her waist, looking down into her dark, watchful eyes. 'I've only known you a few days, Rosanna, but frankly I think the man's mad to go off and leave you for months at a time.'

'David trusts me.'

'Do you trust him?'

She frowned, startled. 'Of course I do,' she said, with rather more force than necessary.

'Do you never wonder what he's doing with his spare time out there in Boston?'

Rosanna detached herself, frowning. 'No,' she said shortly. 'David's other passion is trout fishing, not women. He's not like that.'

'All men are like that.'

'I meant,' she said hotly, 'that if David were seeing someone else he'd say so.'

'I very much doubt it.'

'You don't know him!'

'True.' Ewen gave her a very crooked smile. 'Which is all to the good. I might tell him what a fool he is.'

'David's absolutely nothing to do with you. And his attitude to women is very different from yours,' she snapped, then could have bitten her tongue.

'I see.' He stood back, his face rigid with offence. 'Leave this. I'll make coffee.'

'Thank you.' Dismayed by the sudden hostility in the air, Rosanna gave him a small, conciliatory smile. 'I'm sorry. That was uncalled for. Could I have a piece of your mother's walnut cake with my coffee, please?'

For the rest of the evening Ewen pointedly made no more mention of David. Instead he concentrated on finding out more about Rosanna, and in the process discovered several common interests, including a habit of running at least a couple of miles every day. When they moved on to books eventually the subject led them to the work in hand, which absorbed them both so much that Rosanna was astonished when she realised it was time to go home.

'But after tonight no more cabs. If I'm coming here every day I'll use the Tube,' she said firmly.

'You will not,' contradicted Ewen. 'I forgot to mention that I'll pay for transport. The job's no sinecure, Rosanna. I flatly refuse to let you cope with the Underground after a hard day's work.'

As she prepared for bed later Rosanna decided Ewen's concern for her welfare was very pleasing. David had known her so long he tended to take her self-sufficiency for granted. Which was natural enough, of course. She *could* take care of herself. It was rather nice, just the same, to be taken care of by someone else for a change.

But once her light was out Rosanna found it hard to get to sleep. Ewen's remarks about David had sewn seeds of doubt, and not for the first time since David's departure to America Rosanna began to wonder about his social life there. *Was* there some reason for his failure to come home for a break? David invariably discussed his job during his brief calls, or the trout fishing he was so fond of. He was unfailingly affectionate, sometimes dog-tired, but always the same David. She would write to him tomorrow, thought

Rosanna with sudden purpose, and instead of telling him what she did with her free time ask him about his. And suggest again it was time she went over to see him and share some of it.

Ewen Fraser arranged delivery of a new computer with remarkable speed. It would be delivered that very evening, he informed her when she reported in on her first day.

'Good thing you don't have much furniture,' panted Rosanna as she helped him rearrange the sofas to make room for the leather chairs. 'These spoil the aesthetics in here a bit.'

'Once we get a desk and the other computer in maybe they can go back. For now let's keep the field clear,' said Ewen. 'Have some coffee first, then come out with me to look for a new desk. Are you game for a stroll? There's an auction on at Bonham's.'

'I'm supposed to be working—these jeans aren't very elegant,' she said half-heartedly.

Ewen gave her the look which always made her pulse quicken. 'What does that matter? You look good to me. Besides,' he added, suddenly brisk, 'you'll be the one working at the desk. I want to find one that suits you.'

Rosanna was by no means averse to spending the morning with Ewen. It was very pleasant indeed to stroll along by the Thames along Cheyne Walk in the warm June sunshine. The undercurrent of sexual tension, which was never quite missing beneath the surface, merely added an extra dimension to the morning as they chatted and wrangled together as though they'd known each other years instead of weeks. And Rosanna was utterly fascinated with the famous auction house in Lots Road. They spent an engrossing hour going through furniture of every description, some of it not nearly as valuable, or expensive, as she'd expected. Eventually they settled on a solid Victorian pine table with original leather top and two handy drawers. They spotted a leather captain's chair to go with it, and later on Ewen bid for both items and secured them for only a little more than the reserve price.

By the time they'd eaten the pub lunch Ewen insisted on it was well into the afternoon before they got back to the house, but Rosanna settled at once to some research.

'I'll start as I mean to go on,' she said firmly. 'And you'd better get back to your computer, too, before your muse deserts you.'

'You're in bossy mode again,' complained Ewen.

'That's right. You'd better get used to it. I'll read and make notes down here while you get back to work.'

Rosanna curled up on one of the sofas, and opened the book Ewen asked her to read first. It was quiet outside in the mews, where the houses were occupied in the main by smart young professional couples. Ewen's home was very elegant, decided Rosanna, but she'd still prefer something in the country—a cottage with a garden where children could play. Not that her dream had any hope of coming true for a good few years yet. If ever. Rosanna sighed, and concentrated firmly on the wartime rigours of entrenched Flanders, making notes on a lined pad as she went.

She came to with a start to the touch of Ewen's hand on her shoulder, and looked up at him, blinking owlishly.

'It's six o'clock, Rosanna,' he announced. 'Enough for today.'

'Is it that time already?' She stood up, yawning. 'How are you doing?'

'Very well, surprisingly.' He ran a hand through his hair, stretching mightily. 'I'll see you off, eat something while I wait for the computer, then have an early night. Tomorrow,' he added with relish, 'the real battle begins.'

'I'm looking forward to it.' She yawned again, and he chuckled and patted her shoulder.

'I rang for a cab earlier. It should be here any minute.'

'Thanks. Is nine all right in the morning? I'd like a run first.'

'Whenever you like, Rosanna.' Ewen saw her to the door as the bell rang. 'Get a good night's sleep.' He stretched out a hand suddenly and ruffled her hair, the gesture as intimate as though he'd taken her in his arms and kissed her.

'You too,' she said breathlessly. 'I've enjoyed the day.'

'So have I,' he agreed softly, and Rosanna turned away quickly and ducked into the taxi, before Ewen realised how much she wanted to stay.

After an interval of getting to grips with the unfamiliar computer Rosanna quickly settled into a routine she enjoyed from the first. She began on Ewen's draft, amending errors as she went, checking dates and places and references, her mind soon able to make adjustments and enjoy the story simultaneously, and at the same time leave Ewen free to get on with the actual composition of the novel. And each afternoon they met up for a tea break to discuss the day's work, and give Rosanna the opportunity to ask questions, and point out any discrepancies in the text.

Since Ewen was now working at speed, relieved of any stoppages for reference, he was always way ahead of Rosanna, who worked at a slower pace, paying great attention to detail. But instead of working into the night Ewen began to keep more regular hours, rarely carrying on after Rosanna had gone home, other than to read the corrected drafts she'd printed out for him. And in consequence looked less exhausted and hollow-eyed. And more attractive than ever, thought Rosanna glumly, wondering if her help was giving him more time for a social life.

Her own was non-existent. In the evenings she was invariably too tired to go out, which prompted much argument from Louise, who had sent the newest man of her dreams packing, as predicted.

'You'll turn into a hermit,' warned Louise over the phone. 'All work and no play isn't right, Rosanna Carey. This author of yours is more of a slave-driver than the dreaded Charlie Clayton. On the other hand,' she added curiously, 'maybe it isn't all work. Is there something you're keeping from me? He's supposed to be a bit of a lad with the girls—according to the gossip columns, anyway.'

Rosanna scotched that theory before the idea took root in Louise's brain, making it clear that the job was only temporary, to assist the author to a deadline, and Ewen Fraser wasn't a slave-driver and she thoroughly enjoyed the work. 'His private life is nothing to do with me. And the money he's paying me is *very* generous,' she added.

Louise lost interest in Ewen Fraser and ordered her friend to come to a party at the flat the following weekend, before their friends began to wonder if Rosanna was still on the planet.

'I'm not really in party mood,' began Rosanna, but in the end gave in to Louise's coaxing. 'Oh, all right. Enough. I'll come. How's Paula getting on with the flat-hunting?'

'Not terribly well. She can't seem to find anything suitable.'

'Well, tell her to get a move on,' said Rosanna irritably. 'She's your chum.'

'Gosh, you do sound crotchety,' said Louise. 'Keep your hair on. I'll tell her. In the meantime buy a new dress and be here at eight

on Saturday. I've got some very promising talent lined up.'

Rosanna couldn't raise a flicker of interest
in Louise's so-called 'talent'. No one was
likely to hold a candle to—to David.

When David rang next Rosanna told him
she was now working for an author instead of
Charlie Clayton.

'Just until I start school,' she added brightly.

David, who knew Charlie of old, was un-
surprised to hear she'd packed in her job with
him, and congratulated her on finding an em-
ployer who paid so well. Though Rosanna
knew, in her heart of hearts, that David
wouldn't be quite so pleased if he met Ewen
Fraser in person. Nor was he going to, if she
could possibly manage it.

'I'm earning enough to rise easily to an air
ticket, by the way,' she went on.

'Great!' said David. 'I'm working on some
dates.'

'So I don't interfere with your trout fishing?'

He laughed and promised to give her a definite date next time he rang.

It was later than usual when Rosanna finished on the Friday evening. She went upstairs to the study to find Ewen, eyes glued to the screen and fingers racing over the keyboard, as usual.

'I'm off now, Ewen,' she said loudly.

He swivelled round in his chair, blinking as he thrust a hand through his untidy hair. 'Is it that time already?' He looked at his watch, then scowled. 'No, it damn well isn't. You should have knocked off an hour ago, Rosanna.'

'I wanted to leave off at a suitable point. I've left a pile of pages on the desk for you to look through over the weekend.' She yawned involuntarily, then pulled a face. 'Sorry.'

'I should be sorry, not you. Hang on a minute.' Ewen transferred the day's work to floppy disk, then switched off the machine and got up, smiling at her persuasively. 'Right. Let's have a drink before you go.'

'No, thanks. I must get home.'

'Why? Heavy date tonight?'

'No. I'm a bit tired, that's all. And distinctly scruffy!' Rosanna smiled. 'I need a bath and a good night's sleep. I'm bidden to a party to-morrow.'

Ewen followed her down the stairs. 'Is that allowed?'

'Allowed?'

'Doesn't the doctor object?'

'Why should he? It's something to write about in my next letter,' she said shortly, and slung her bag over her shoulder.

'Did you write about the time you dined with me?' Ewen asked abruptly.

'I told him about you, yes.'

'And he doesn't mind?'

'No.'

Ewen shook his head. 'A bit of a saint, this doctor of yours, Rosanna. I can't say I'd be so understanding in the same circumstances.'

'I didn't tell him I'd been out with you,' she admitted reluctantly. 'Just about working for you.'

'Ah!' Ewen caught her by the elbows and drew her towards him. 'Why was that, I wonder?'

Rosanna's eyes dropped. 'As it won't happen again I saw no reason to mention it. That's my taxi. Goodnight. I'll see you Monday.' She pulled away and walked to the door.

'One moment, Rosanna.' He opened the door for her. 'Thank you for all your hard work. I'm grateful. By the way, where's the party?'

'At my very own flat. Friend Louise thinks I'm in danger of turning into a hermit.' Rosanna smiled. 'She's sorted out some men she thinks I'll find interesting.'

'And will you?'

'I won't know until I meet them!'

It was strange to go back to the flat like a visitor the following evening. Rosanna used her key to let herself into an atmosphere thick with cigarette smoke, the small sitting room crammed wall to wall with people talking at the tops of their voices above the strident music.

'*Rosanna*,' screeched Louise, who came pushing through the crowd in a see-through dress over what appeared to be a matching girdle and bra. Her blonde hair was carefully arranged to look as if she'd been out in a force-nine gale, and she was obviously having the time of her life. 'You're late,' she accused. 'Come and meet Dominic and Eddy.'

Rosanna had fallen back on the little black dress again. She felt like a dowdy sparrow in a pen of peacocks as her friend towed her through the throng towards two elegant young men. Louise thrust a glass into her hand, introduced her, then left her to make conversation. Eddy was an actor, Dominic in advertising, both of them obviously much more interested in each other than in Rosanna. After a while she left them to it, and went to talk to people she knew. But to her dismay she soon found she was bored. Yet not so long before she would have been the life and soul of a party like this. She pulled herself together and did her utmost to sparkle, right up to the moment when the exquisite Eddy appeared in a blonde wig and one of Louise's dresses to give his Dolly Parton imitation.

'What's up?' hissed Louise when Rosanna told her she was leaving.

'Headache,' she lied. 'I'll ring you tomorrow.'

Rosanna arrived home, wondering what on earth was wrong with her. Leaving a party halfway through was a first. Especially when there was nothing at all to get home for.

Her only consolation was the winking red light on the telephone. She pushed the button eagerly, then sat down abruptly in the hall chair, appalled at the depth of her disappointment.

'Out with your lover again?' asked David cheerfully. 'I just rang to tell you I'm off this weekend, fishing again, so don't call back. I'll ring you on Monday with the dates I promised.'

A second message was from her mother. 'Glad you're out on Saturday night, darling. We may be staying on a while longer, but I'll ring you tomorrow morning your time for a chat. Dad sends his love.'

After hearing her mother's voice Rosanna felt more blue than ever. But when a third message began she sprang to her feet, her spirits suddenly soaring.

'Ewen here, Rosanna. I'm a bit stuck with the last part of the draft you did yesterday. Can you call me when you get in? I don't mind how late it is. I can't get on until I talk to you. Did you have a good time at your party?'

Rosanna dialled Ewen's number at once, then could have kicked herself when she heard the surprise in his voice.

'Rosanna? Why are you home so early? What's wrong?'

'Nothing. I just wasn't in party mood.'

'You were too damn tired,' he said forcibly. 'I've been working you too hard.'

'No, you haven't,' she retorted. 'You throw me out on the stroke of six whether I've finished or not.'

'That's never because I want you to go, Rosanna.' The deepened, caressing note in his voice curled her toes in her strappy suede shoes.

She took in a deep breath. 'Anyway, you don't work me too hard. Tonight I just didn't feel like partying, I suppose.'

'Does that happen often?'

'Oh, yes,' she lied shamelessly.

'What about the company your friend was laying on for you?'

'Love at first sight—with each other!'

Ewen laughed. 'Commiserations.'

'So what's the problem?'

'Problem?'

'With the draft,' she said patiently.

'Ah.' He paused. 'Actually there isn't a problem. I just wanted to know when you got home.'

Rosanna sat down again. 'Why?'

'I worry about you all alone in that house. I imagined some Romeo taking you home and trying—'

'Now then, Ewen,' she said sweetly. 'Don't judge everyone by yourself.'

'I don't. That's the trouble. Most men would have tried to take things a damn sight further than I did, Rosanna.'

Her mouth curved in a small, secretive smile. 'Please don't take this as a challenge, Ewen Fraser, but why the restraint?'

'You won't like it.'

'Tell me just the same.'

'I was tempted almost beyond endurance, but I still couldn't forget you were Rose's granddaughter.'

She sighed. 'I thought so. If I'd been some-one else's grandchild you'd have tried to take me to bed.'

'And succeeded.'

'Oh, really?'

'Yes, really!' he mocked. 'But you are who you are and I'm Harry's great-nephew, so there we are. Checkmate.'

'There are other reasons,' she retorted. 'David for one.'

'Ah, yes. The doctor. I tend to forget him.'

'I don't. I'm going to marry him,' she said tartly.

'Ah, but when, Rosanna? This year, next year, sometime—?'

'When the time's right,' she snapped, so crossly Ewen chuckled.

'All right, Rosanna, I won't tease you any more. I'm just glad to know you're home safe and sound. See you Monday.'

CHAPTER SIX

WHEN the call came through from Australia next day Rosanna assured her mother she was quite happy to carry on house-sitting indefinitely.

'Paula hasn't found anywhere else suitable yet, so she's paying my share to Louise and I'm living here rent-free, plus the very generous money Ewen Fraser pays me. My finances are in good shape for once.'

'Ah, yes. Ewen Fraser. How do you like working for him, darling?'

Rosanna assured her mother the work was utterly fascinating, almost enough to make up for her own disappointment. 'I was so sure I could write,' she said ruefully. 'But now I read Ewen's story day by day I realise I could never achieve anything remotely similar.'

In actual fact, working for Ewen had developed into a routine so pleasurable, routine was entirely the wrong word to describe it.

Rosanna found the whole process of helping him so absorbing that she resented two whole days spent away from it at the weekend, and sometimes felt annoyed with Ewen when he called a halt each day, promptly at six, sometimes well before she wanted to finish.

'Don't flash those eyes of yours at me,' he warned, one such evening. 'It's time to go home.'

'I'd rather stay just until—'

'No,' he said inexorably. 'If your parents come home to find you looking worn to shreds I'll get the blame.'

'Do I look so terrible, then?' she demanded, closing down the computer.

'No,' he said curtly. 'You don't. And you're not going to on my account.' He walked with her to the door, eyeing her thoughtfully. 'Rosanna, could you bring yourself to do me a great favour?'

'If I can,' she said warily. 'What is it?'

'Are you by any chance free on Sunday?'

Her eyes narrowed. 'Why?'

'My mother desires my presence at a lunch party.' He smiled down at her coaxingly. 'Come with me, Rosanna.'

She stared at him, astonished. 'Am I allowed to ask why?'

Ewen shrugged. 'I need protective cover. One of the guests invited tends to come on a bit strong these days since my modest success.'

'Man or woman?' asked Rosanna, grinning.

'A man would be easier. He wouldn't want to marry me.'

'Oh, dear—the fate worse than death again. You need a minder!'

'No. A companion.' He moved nearer. 'Will you come?'

Rosanna thought it over. A lunch party with a lot of people was harmless enough, surely. 'Do your people know my connection to Harry—and Rose?'

'Of course they do. They're very anxious to meet you.'

She smiled, capitulating. 'All right. What shall I wear?'

Ewen's eyes gleamed triumphantly. 'Anything you like. I'll pick you up about twelve.'

Rosanna spent Saturday with Louise, who whistled, astonished, when she heard Ewen Fraser was taking her to a family party.

'Well, well,' she said with relish. 'Does David know?'

'It's not that kind of thing at all. I'm just going along as Ewen's cover.'

'Cover for what?'

'He's having trouble with some woman who wants his body now he's got money.'

Louise regarded her friend with sparkling eyes. 'Is his body worth having, then?' She stared, astonished. 'Lordy, lordy, Rosanna Carey. Is that a blush?'

'Certainly not. I never blush.'

'Normally no. I'd kill for that creamy skin of yours. But you definitely changed colour just then.'

Rosanna hastily diverted Louise by asking for help to find a dress for the lunch party. And quickly regretted it. Louise's taste inclined to the spectacular, and she was frankly disparaging about Rosanna's choice of a sleeveless shift in sea-blue linen.

'Perfect for making a hit with his family,' she agreed, grudgingly. 'But something slinkier would have been better for frightening off the competition.'

Rosanna got home late, tired after Louise's idea of an action-packed day. She would have liked to check with Ewen if her gift of Charbonnel & Walker chocolates was to his mother's taste. But there was no message from him this time. And she was disappointed. So much so that when David rang as she was going to bed, giving her the choice of dates in early August for her trip, she was a lot more demonstrative than usual. He was surprised, and asked why.

'I miss you,' she said emphatically, and later, after she'd put the phone down, she repeated to her reflection, 'I do miss David. A lot.'

Rosanna woke to a Sunday of hot, cloudless sunshine, slightly nervous at the prospect of meeting Ewen's parents. He rang during the morning to say he would collect her at twelve, and she would need something to tie over her hair.

Intrigued, Rosanna found a blue-striped yellow scarf of her mother's, hoping it wouldn't cause havoc with her hair. She had left it loose to soften the effect of the severely plain dress, and felt quite pleased with the result as she opened the door at Ewen's ring.

But it wasn't Ewen. A tanned, scowling young man brushed past her into the hall, brandishing an envelope.

'Hello, Charlie,' she said, resigned. 'Had a nice time?'

'What the hell is this, Rosanna?' he demanded.

'You can read, Charlie. It's my resignation. I told you about it before you went on holiday.'

'I never thought you were serious!'

'Because you didn't listen. Where's Helen?'

'I dropped her off at her mother's to dish out presents, and so on—but never mind that,' he said irritably. 'I refuse to accept this. I insist you stay until I find someone else.'

'Do you, now?' said Rosanna, eyes flashing. 'Look here, Charlie, I only helped you out as a favour.'

'I paid you a salary!' he said, injured.

'A pittance, you mean,' she snapped. 'Out of the goodness of my heart I toiled for days after you left to clear everything up. But you can have all that for free. You'd have to get someone else soon, anyway, when I start teaching again.'

'Oh, come on, Rosanna; be a sport and come back until then, at least!'

'No can do, I'm afraid.' She glanced at her watch. 'Sorry to rush you, but I'm going out. Give my love to Helen.'

'You've got a nerve!'

'That's rich, coming from you, Charlie,' she retorted. 'You're the one with nerve. A word of advice. When you find my replacement, pay her more, iron your own shirts and make your own lunch.'

'All right, all right. You've made your point.' He summoned up a coaxing smile. 'Look, Rosie, at least stay until I find someone else. I suppose I can scrape up a bit more money.'

'It's not a question of money, Charlie. Call an agency and get a temp. I'm working for someone else until term starts.'

Charlie grabbed her by the shoulders and turned her to face him, glaring down at her. 'What the hell's got into you? I thought we were friends—'

'Is anything wrong, Rosanna?' said a menacing voice from the doorway.

Charlie's hands dropped, his face flushing as he turned to confront an openly hostile Ewen Fraser.

Rosanna's smile was radiant with relief. 'Ewen, you're on time. Let me introduce you. Ewen Fraser, Charlie Clayton.'

Ewen nodded curtly.

'Hi,' muttered Charlie.

'We must be going,' said Rosanna firmly. 'Goodbye, Charlie. Tell Helen I'll ring her.'

'How's David?' he asked deliberately.

'He's fine. Working hard. I'll tell him you asked.' Rosanna propelled Charlie to the door, said her goodbyes and closed it behind him, then leaned against it, blowing out her cheeks.

'Are you all right?' demanded Ewen, seizing her hands. 'My gut reaction was to haul the jerk off and thump him. But it could have been David, for all I knew.'

'Charlie's an old college mate, a bit hot-tempered, but harmless enough.' Rosanna pulled a face. 'My notice didn't go down well. He was trying to persuade me to go back to him.'

'I gathered that.' Ewen released her hands abruptly. 'Did he succeed?'

'You know very well he didn't,' she retorted.

Ewen reached out to touch her cheek. 'I'm glad.' He smiled crookedly and moved back. 'Sorry. Not in the contract.'

Rosanna resisted the urge to put a hand to the place he'd touched and turned away to eye her reflection. 'Will I do?'

Ewen looked her over with unhurried, relishing scrutiny. 'I just hope the journey doesn't spoil such ravishing perfection.'

'Why should it?' she asked curiously as she locked up.

'I've brought the Morgan.'

The green two-seater sports car stood at the kerb, the distinctive style so little changed over the years that one look at it shrieked its origins. Rosanna's eyes sparkled with amusement as Ewen ran a possessive, caressing hand over the bonnet.

'She's very beautiful,' said Rosanna with suitable respect, and tied the scarf over her hair, secretly praying she wouldn't look a total wreck by the time they got to his parents' house.

'I always hankered for one of these. When I began earning a bit from my writing I placed my order right away, but I had to wait four long years for her,' said Ewen, handing Rosanna into the passenger seat. He looked down into her face. 'But I'm a patient man. All things come to those who wait.'

The words evoked a shiver somewhere in the region of Rosanna's blue linen midriff, and she put sunglasses on to hide any similar reaction on her face. He looked good himself today, she admitted secretly. His dark hair gleamed with copper lights in the noon sunlight, and he wore a light blue shirt with the pale linen suit she'd seen before. He might not be possessed of movie star looks, but there was something about him that stirred a response inside her she'd never felt for anyone since meeting David. Ewen Fraser possessed an indefinable charisma which far outshone mere good looks. Something to guard against by remembering the other women who'd fallen victim to it.

'We match,' she commented, flicking a finger at her blue dress.

He slanted a significant look at her. 'I know.'

'My dress is new. I bought it yesterday,' she said, unruffled. 'I hope it's right for the purpose.'

'If you mean for charming my parents—'

'I meant for frightening off lady predators,' she retorted.

Ewen laughed as he threaded the Morgan through the traffic. 'Perfect for that, too.' He glanced at the gold rose pinned to her shoulder. 'I see you're wearing the brooch again.'

Rosanna nodded. 'My flatmate Louise vetoed my pearls. Too dull for words, she told me. My taste in clothes invariably disappoints her.'

'It doesn't disappoint me!'

'Thank you. Where are we headed?'

'My parents moved into one of those riverside flats a few years ago.'

Rosanna couldn't hide her tension when Ewen eventually drove into the car park of a building converted from warehouse origins into stylish apartments.

'I'm nervous,' she confessed in the lift.

'Of meeting my parents?'

She nodded, fiddling with the posy slotted through the ribbon bow on the chocolates.

'Why?'

'Because they know about Rose.'

The lift glided to a halt, and Ewen took her hand as they stepped out onto a quiet hall at the top of the building. 'Don't worry. I'll keep you safe,' he whispered, and pressed the bell on one of the doors.

The woman who opened it to them was enough like her son to need no introduction. After Ewen had kissed her she gazed at Rosanna in silence for a moment, then smiled apologetically and held out her hand. 'Do forgive me, my dear. Ewen did warn me, but the resemblance to your grandmother's photograph is quite startling. Welcome, Rosanna. I'm Mary Fraser.'

'It's very kind of you to invite me.' Rosanna returned the smile, and held out the offering. 'I hoped you'd have a sweet tooth.'

'I do indeed,' said Mrs Fraser warmly, 'but my mother's is sweeter still. Why not give the chocolates to her, instead? Come and meet my husband.'

Alec Fraser's only resemblance to his son was the hair, iron-grey but still luxuriant, which had obviously once been like Ewen's. He greeted Rosanna warmly, in accents which still retained their unmissable Edinburgh flavour, and took her into a large room with a magnificent view of the river. The room was packed, but there was a drop in the level of noise for a moment as Ewen placed a hand under Rosanna's elbow and propelled her towards a very elderly lady seated in a high-backed chair.

'Hello, Grandma,' said Ewen, and knelt by her chair to hug her. He took a small package from his pocket and handed it to her. 'Happy birthday.'

Rosanna stiffened. Birthday?

'My favourite perfume,' said his grandmother in approval. 'Good boy. Thank you, Ewen.'

'This is Rosanna Carey,' he said rather loudly.

'No need to shout,' said the old lady. Her eyes, hazel like Ewen's, lingered appreciatively on Rosanna's face. 'No need for an introduction, either. You're Rose Norman's granddaughter.'

Rosanna nodded shyly. 'Yes, I am. How do you do?' She proffered the chocolates. 'Ewen didn't tell me it was your birthday. Will you accept these with my good wishes?'

'With pleasure, my dear. I adore chocolates. At ninety,' added the birthday girl with a twinkle, 'chocolate is the only sin left to me.'

Rosanna laughed, feeling more at ease, her fleeting anger with Ewen subsiding when he told his grandmother he was stealing Rosanna to introduce her to everyone before lunch. 'Afterwards,' he promised, 'I'll bring her back and you can talk to her as long as you like.'

He was as good as his word. With an arm linked through Rosanna's he introduced her to a selection of uncles, aunts, cousins and family friends, until her head was reeling by the time Mary Fraser came to the rescue.

'For heaven's sake give the poor girl a drink, Ewen.' She smiled at Rosanna with sympathy. 'I hope you're not too overwhelmed with Frasers and Hiltons.'

Rosanna was provided with a glass of wine, then drawn into a group of Ewen's contemporaries. They were all friendly and welcoming except for the woman who sailed across the room to seize Ewen by the shoulders and give him a lingering kiss. She was tall, with expensively cut red hair, and opulent curves displayed to advantage in the type of dress Louise had urged Rosanna to buy. Printed chiffon over a nude underslip gave the startling impression that the lady was wearing only a few scattered flowers.

'Darling!' she said, hooking her arm in Ewen's. 'Where have you *been*? I've missed you horribly.'

'Working hard, Geraldine,' he assured her. 'Let me introduce you to Rosanna Carey.'

Geraldine turned a baulked, green gaze on the girl Ewen held firmly by the waist. 'Hello,' she said indifferently, and turned her attention back to Ewen. 'You never answer my calls, you heartbreaker. You can't be busy all the time.'

'I've got a deadline to meet,' he said smoothly, and with faultless manners chatted pleasantly for a moment or two. 'Forgive me, Gerry,' he said eventually. 'Must circulate.' He detached her scarlet-tipped hand, kissed it gallantly, then took Rosanna to join a group of cousins who teased him unmercifully about his new celebrity status.

'Is he a pig to work for?' asked one of the young women.

'No, not at all.' Rosanna smiled demurely up at Ewen. 'He's shut in his study upstairs all day, and I work downstairs.'

'But we meet occasionally over the lunch-time sandwiches—which I get delivered,' added Ewen, grinning down at her.

Rosanna found she was enjoying herself, and soon discovered that more eyes than the spectacular Geraldine's were turned in Ewen's direction. Every woman in the room, young or old, related or not, responded to the charm he made no conscious effort to exert. It was a very relaxed, lively gathering who eventually enjoyed lunch served from a lavish buffet. Ewen's grandmother was given a special tray, and made much of, to her obvious delight. When everyone toasted her in champagne later, and sang 'Happy Birthday', she blew kisses in all directions, then gave Ewen an imperious wave.

'You've been summoned,' said Ewen, escorting Rosanna across the room. 'Grandma wants a chat. Do you mind if I leave you with her for a while?'

'No. But take care,' she muttered in an undertone. 'Geraldine's hovering, ready to pounce.'

He smothered a laugh, provided Rosanna with a footstool at his grandmother's knee, then went off to help his mother pass out slices of birthday cake, an adroit manoeuvre which kept him out of Geraldine's clutches very neatly.

Clever devil, thought Rosanna, not for the first time. 'It's a lovely party, Mrs Hilton,' she said aloud.

The old lady patted her cheek, smiling. 'My dear, let me introduce myself properly. Hard to believe now, I know, but I'm Harry Manners' baby sister. Harry showed me Rose's photograph long ago, when I was very young.'

'Oh. I see,' said Rosanna huskily.

The keen old eyes misted a little. 'I was desperate to marry some unsuitable fellow. Harry was ten years my senior, very much the professional soldier by that time. And very reserved. But to save me from a terrible mistake he confided in me; told me why he'd never married.' Mrs Hilton shrugged ruefully. 'It made my little romance seem very tawdry. And not long afterwards I met the real love of my life, and Harry, bless him, never even said "I told you so".'

Rosanna clasped her hands round her knees, deeply moved. 'Thank you so much for telling me. Have you read Rose's diary and letters?'

'Certainly not, my dear.' The old lady leaned to pat Rosanna's hand. 'Harry left them to Ewen. He was very fond of the boy. I'll wait until the book comes out,' she added naughtily, and Rosanna chuckled.

'It's worth waiting for, I promise.'

'Do you like my grandson?' asked Mrs Hilton without warning.

Rosanna blinked, startled. 'Why, yes—yes, I do.'

'So do I.' The old lady beckoned to Ewen. 'We're getting a bit maudlin. Take Rosanna back to the others, and ask Mary to make me a cup of tea before I go.'

'Go?' said Rosanna, jumping up.

'I live in a retirement home, my dear,' said Mrs Hilton, chuckling. 'Five-star accommodation, my own room, television and video recorder. Which I know how to operate, too,' she said smugly. 'Come and visit me there. Ewen can bring you.'

People were beginning to leave, and Ewen was helping his parents see them off when Rosanna found herself alone with an attractive, fair-haired young woman who'd arrived late.

'I'm Nicola Blake,' she said, holding out her hand. 'I've just arrived home on holiday, nearly missed the party.'

Rosanna took the hand, smiling. 'I'm Rosanna Carey. Are you a cousin, too?'

'Not exactly. My sister Priscilla over there married Ewen's cousin Mark. I made the effort today because it was Mrs Hilton's ninetieth birthday. I felt I couldn't miss it. She's such a grand old lady.'

Rosanna liked Nicola Blake on sight, and would have been happy to chat with her for a while, but Ewen joined them quickly, his face wary.

'Hello, Nicola. Better late then never.'

She smiled brightly. 'Just got back from foreign parts, Ewen. I couldn't let jet-lag keep me away on your grandmother's special day.'

'Very kind of you. You've met Rosanna?' asked Ewen.

'We introduced ourselves,' said Rosanna, looking from one expressionless face to the other. 'We discovered we were kindred spirits.'

'In what way?' he said sharply.

Nicola smiled at him. 'We seem to be the only non-relatives at the party.' She finished her wine and handed him the empty glass. 'I must be going. Nice to meet you, Rosanna. I'll just have a word with your parents, Ewen, then I'll beg a lift from Priscilla and Mark. Goodbye.'

'Who was that?' asked Rosanna, in the little silence that followed Nicola's departure.

'An old friend,' he said dismissively. 'Mother wants us to stay on for a while when everyone's gone. Says she hasn't had a chance to chat. All right with you?'

'Yes, of course.'

'Just a half-hour or so,' he promised.

It was a good deal longer than that by the time Mrs Hilton had been seen off, and everyone, even the reluctant Geraldine, had finally gone. And the moment the elder Frasers had Rosanna to themselves her resemblance to her grandmother was the main topic of conversation, along with Ewen's good fortune in tracking down Rose Norman's family to learn her story. By that time the sky had grown dark and thunder was beginning to rumble across the river. Ewen turned down the offer of supper.

'I'd better get Rosanna home before the storm breaks. I work her hard,' he said lightly, kissing his mother. 'She needs her sleep.'

'Perhaps you should hang on until the weather improves,' said his father as lightning lit up the room.

'Thanks just the same, but I'd better get home,' said Rosanna. 'I like storms.' She smiled at Ewen. 'I assume the hood doesn't leak on your prized possession?'

'Certainly not!'

They made their farewells, and at last, when the lift doors closed behind them, Ewen braced himself, eyeing her warily. 'You look a touch militant, Rosanna.'

'As well I might,' she said promptly. 'You didn't say it was your grandmother's birthday, or exactly how much feminine attention I was required to shield you from.' She looked at him challengingly. 'Who, exactly, is Nicola—?' She gasped, choking back a scream as the lights went out and the lift stopped dead.

Ewen fumbled for her hand. 'Are you all right?'

'No!' She hurled herself into his arms, clinging to him like a limpet. 'Don't you have a match or something?'

Ewen cursed under his breath. 'I don't smoke. Let me feel for the control panel. There must be a panic button—'

'Don't mention panic!' she implored, and he laughed, patting her back soothingly.

'It must be the lightning. But don't worry. Someone will soon put it right.'

'But it's Sunday night!' she wailed.

'Which is where emergency services come in.' He cursed again. 'Nothing doing with any of these buttons. There's no phone in here either. I'm afraid we just wait. Don't worry, my father'll be on the case as we speak.' Ewen settled her more comfortably in his arms. 'I thought you weren't afraid of storms,' he teased.

'I'm not,' she said hoarsely. 'Claustrophobia's my problem. I loathe lifts even when they're moving.'

Ewen's arms tightened, and she clung to him convulsively. 'At this moment I can't say I loathe them myself,' he said breathlessly. 'Let's think of some way to pass the time. No point in "I spy", I'm afraid.'

Rosanna gave a hysterical little chuckle. 'Talk to me, Ewen. Take my mind off it somehow. *Please!*'

'This is the best way.' He turned her face up to his, finding her mouth unerringly in the darkness. For a moment she resisted, but sheer visceral fear cancelled out normal caution, and she responded to him with fervour, passionately grateful for the security of Ewen's embrace. But security quickly changed to danger. Rosanna gasped as Ewen's tongue penetrated her mouth, twining with hers in a caress so intimate and inflaming her knees trembled and she melted against him as he held her so tightly their hearts thumped in a united drumbeat, urging the blood through her veins.

Ewen held her with one hand as he shrugged off his jacket, then pushed Rosanna against the wall of the lift, his body holding her there as he caressed her bare arms, and her throat, thrusting his hands through the heavy waves of her hair as he kissed her with such unrestrained passion, Rosanna forgot they were imprisoned in a lift, forgot everything in the surge of response which bathed her entire body in fire as she stood on tiptoe and wreathed her arms around Ewen's taut neck. Breathing raggedly, he bent his head to kiss her throat, his hands reaching behind her to undo her zip and slide her dress off her shoulders.

Rosanna thrust herself against him shamelessly, and Ewen gave a deep-throated sound of mingled pain and pleasure as he kissed her with escalating hunger, his hands moving over her in the darkness, learning every curving contour with his fingertips. The tortured, unsteady rhythm of their breathing was loud in the enclosed space as Rosanna astonished herself by undoing Ewen's shirt to press openmouthed kisses against the taut muscles of his bare chest.

Ewen let out another groan and crushed her against him, then slid to the floor, cradling her in his lap. He caressed her with shaking hands, and she arched her back involuntarily as his lips found her bared breasts, his teeth grazing with exquisite skill at the tips. Streaks of sweet agony shot through her. Secret, inner muscles contracted as his fingers slid slowly up her parted thighs, and she gave a smothered moan, her entire body on fire with anticipation.

Then the lights came on and the lift began to move downwards.

With a muffled curse Ewen shot to his feet, hauling Rosanna with him. With shaking hands she fastened her bra, then snatched her dress into place, turning her back for him to close the zip. She thrust her feet into her discarded shoes, then stared in horror when Ewen stabbed a finger at a button and sent the lift up again as it reached the basement.

'What are you *doing*?' she demanded, rummaging frantically in her bag for a comb.

'My parents are probably going mad up there,' he panted as he thrust his shirt back under his belt.

'You mean I've got to face them looking like this?' She raked the comb through her hair, gasping for breath.

'You look beautiful,' he said hoarsely. 'And I want you like hell.'

Rosanna gave him a glare of angry panic, then the doors opened and Mary Fraser rushed to hug her.

'Oh, my dears, I've been going out of my mind!'

'So has Rosanna,' said Ewen, thrusting a hand through his hair. 'Claustrophobia,' he added succinctly.

'You need drinks,' said Alec Fraser. 'I raised the alarm straight away, but it took longer than usual to get the power on.'

Mary Fraser kept her arm round Rosanna as they went back in the flat. 'What can I give you, dear?'

'Tea, please,' said Rosanna breathlessly as Ewen stared at his watch. 'How long were we in there?'

'Twenty minutes.' He gave her a smouldering look. 'It seemed less than that.'

'If Rosanna's claustrophobic,' said his mother tartly, 'I imagine it felt like hours. I'll get that tea.'

Rosanna escaped to a bathroom, and stared at her reflection in dismay. Her hair was reasonable, but her linen dress had suffered badly from its cavalier treatment, and her eyes burned in her pale face. And to anyone with half an eye it was obvious that she'd been kissed half to death. She applied lipstick with an unsteady hand, then squared her shoulders and went back to join the others. Ewen was on the balcony with his father, watching the storm die away, and Mary Fraser beckoned her to a sofa, and began pouring tea.

'Come and sit down, dear. What a way to end the day!'

Rosanna sank down gratefully, smiling valiantly as Ewen and Alec came to join them. 'I'm afraid I was in a terrible state, shut up in there. Ewen had to cuddle me to stop me from banging my head on the wall.'

Alec Fraser laughed, and handed his son a large brandy. 'I bet he hated that!'

'It's a terrible thing, claustrophobia,' said his wife with feeling. 'Mother suffers from it. I just hope *she* wasn't in a lift when the storm broke.'

'We'd have known by now!' said Alec dryly.

They all laughed and Rosanna drank her tea gratefully, suddenly so weary it was an effort to hold the teacup. Ewen accepted another brandy from his father, shaking his head at the look Rosanna gave him.

'Don't worry. I'll take you home in a taxi. They're in demand tonight in this weather, but I was promised one in half an hour.'

'Ewen doesn't like exposing his beloved car to the elements,' said his mother, smiling.

'For once I wasn't concerned about the Morgan, Mother, dear,' he said dryly. 'After our little adventure down there in the lift shaft I really needed a brandy for once.'

'Are you sure you wouldn't like one too, Rosanna?' said Alec Fraser, eyeing her. 'You look very pale.'

She shook her head, smiling, and held out her cup. 'More tea, but no brandy, thank you. Otherwise I won't be fit for work tomorrow.'

'I'm sure Ewen would give you the day off!'

'I won't need it,' said Rosanna firmly.

There was a wry twist to Ewen's lips as he handed her the refilled teacup. 'Your usual run in the park on course as well?'

'I may give that a miss for once,' she conceded, beginning to yearn for her bed.

It was a relief when the intercom rang to announce a taxi for Fraser.

'Are you sure about the lift?' said Ewen after they'd said their goodnights for the second time. 'We could go down the stairs.'

Rosanna pulled a face. 'If I do I may never get in a lift again.'

Nevertheless it was a trial to find herself in an enclosed space again so soon, her tension worsened by Ewen's impenetrable silence which, to her dismay, lasted all the way home in the taxi. When they arrived he asked the taxi driver to wait, and followed Rosanna inside.

She switched on lights and turned to face him in the hall. 'See you in the morning.'

'So you are coming, then?'

'Of course I am. I meant what I said.' She forced her eyes to meet his. 'Nothing happened today to merit time off.'

'Really? Thanks a lot. You certainly know how to cut a man down to size.' Ewen's eyes glittered in his taut face. 'Goodnight, then, Rosanna. Thank you for coming with me today.'

'My pleasure. Any time you want protection from your adoring female public, just say the word,' she said tartly.

'There was only one,' he snapped. 'Geraldine wasn't interested when I was a cub reporter, so she married money. Now she's divorced and I'm successful she's after me again. Money talks.'

'Geraldine wants your body, not your money,' said Rosanna scornfully. 'And she wasn't the only one. There was more than one pair of female eyes lusting after you, Ewen

Fraser. Some of them attached to respectable wedding rings at that! Which reminds me. Who, exactly, is Nicola Blake?'

Ewen looked uncomfortable. 'She's the one who said I was married to my computer. We lived together for a while, but, as I told you, it didn't work out.'

'It didn't work out because she wanted to marry you, not just live with you.' Rosanna eyed him with hostility, surprised to feel sympathy for Nicola Blake. 'In fact, Geraldine was just a decoy, wasn't she? It was Nicola you wanted protection from. She's still in love with you.'

His jaw tightened, but he made no attempt to deny it. 'I made it clear from the start that marriage was never an option. It was a mistake to let Nicola move in with me. I don't deny that. But in common with the majority of my sex I like women. And they tend to reciprocate.'

'And how! I saw that for myself today.' Rosanna paused, then forced herself to say what had to be said. 'Ewen, I'm sorry I made such a fuss afterwards. In the lift, I mean.'

'I'm not sorry. For anything,' he added, and seized her by the elbows suddenly. 'I never thought I'd have cause to be grateful to a storm.' He bent his head and kissed her hard, then released her so suddenly, Rosanna rocked on her heels as he strode from the house to the waiting taxi.

CHAPTER SEVEN

ROSANNA'S tension increased by the minute as she travelled to Chelsea next day. After picking her way over the damp cobbles to Ewen's door she almost turned tail and went home again, but in the end rang the bell, bracing herself for confrontation in the cold light of a wet Monday morning.

Ewen took a long time to come to the door. When he finally appeared, barefoot, wearing only a pair of ancient jeans, she stared at him in horror, forgetting all her qualms.

'Ewen, you look *awful*. Are you ill?'

'No. Hangover.' His eyes, narrowed to malevolent slits, glared from a haggard, ashen face.

She sidled past him warily. 'Anything I can do?'

He shook his head, gasped in agony at the movement, and retreated upstairs to his bedroom without a word.

Rosanna sighed as she gazed after him, then went to fill the coffee machine. After a tactful interval she ran upstairs to knock on Ewen's bedroom door, and at his faint noise of assent entered the room she'd never been inside before. The curtains were drawn, and through the gloom she could just make out the large bed where Ewen lay like an effigy on a tomb.

'Shall I bring you some coffee?' Rosanna enquired.

'Not in the contract,' he muttered.

She went back downstairs, filled a tall beaker with strong black coffee and took it back to Ewen's room. 'Drink that,' she ordered, and put it on the table beside the bed.

Ewen sat up with infinite care, and Rosanna leaned over and stacked pillows behind him. 'Thank you,' he said, without opening his eyes.

'Drink the coffee,' she repeated.

'After you've gone.'

Rosanna left and went downstairs to start work, but concentration was difficult with one ear open for sounds from upstairs. Soon afterwards she heard Ewen race for the bathroom.

Coffee had obviously been a bad idea. She went into the kitchen and took a litre bottle of water from the fridge, found a glass, and went upstairs to find Ewen back in bed.

'You look like death,' she informed him.

One hostile eye opened a fraction. 'Go *away*, Rosanna.'

'All right. I brought you some water this time. Please drink some. You're dehydrated.'

'Quite possibly. Now *go!*'

Rosanna went, determined to ignore the sufferer, and get on with the work he was paying her for. After a while, as always, the force of his writing drew her in, and she was soon oblivious of anything other than the young platoon commander inching his way across no man's land to bring back his wounded corporal. Rosanna became so absorbed she was only torn away by the daily lunch delivery. She took the sandwiches into the kitchen, eyeing them thoughtfully, but decided against taking any up to Ewen, in no mood to get her head bitten off again.

Rosanna made herself a mug of tea, then perched on a kitchen stool with her tuna salad sandwich, and began to read the newspaper she'd bought earlier.

'Sorry I was so rude,' said a voice from the door, and Rosanna turned to find Ewen, dressed and newly shaved, but still pale and haggard.

'That's all right,' she said cheerfully. 'How do you feel?'

'That with care I might just possibly survive.'

'Good.' Rosanna eyed him warily. 'Will you hit me if I offer food?'

He closed his eyes briefly. 'Please. Don't mention food.'

'Tea, then.'

'Tea sounds great.'

'Right.' Rosanna slid from the stool. 'Go back to bed. I'll bring the tea when it's ready.'

'I'm not noble enough to refuse,' he muttered. 'Thank you, Rosanna.'

Rosanna set a tray, added biscuits and a couple of painkillers, then took it upstairs to Ewen's room. This time the curtains were drawn back a little, and Ewen sat propped up against the brass bedhead.

'My angel of mercy,' he said sardonically.

She shrugged. 'I've treated hangovers before.'

'Yours or the good doctor's?'

'My brother's actually—in his wilder days.'

Ewen looked morose. 'I suppose a doctor treats his own hangovers.'

'Try to eat some biscuits and swallow a couple of pills with your tea,' she said briskly, and paused in the doorway. 'What do you normally do for hangovers?'

'Avoid them,' he said bitterly. 'But last night, just for once, I felt like another brandy or two when I got home. So there it is. Crime and punishment.' His eyes speared hers. 'You know why.'

It was late afternoon when Ewen came downstairs again. He stood behind Rosanna for a moment, following what she was reading on the screen, then asked very politely if he could return the compliment and make her some tea.

'Thank you. That would be very nice,' she muttered abstractedly, her eyes glued to the screen. After a while she realised Ewen was still standing behind her and turned round, her eyebrows raised.

'I suppose I should be flattered you find my prose so absorbing.' He stalked off to the kitchen, shutting the door behind him.

Rosanna scowled. There was no pleasing Ewen today. Unlike last night. She hugged her arms suddenly across her chest. Last night, in the lift, she had pleased him far too much. And pleasure didn't begin to describe the feelings Ewen had aroused in return. All day she had worked hard to keep the thought of them at bay, but now the scene came flooding back, and suddenly she buried her face in her hands.

'What's the matter?' demanded Ewen, putting a beaker down beside her.

Rosanna raised her head quickly, running a hand through her hair. 'I've been concentrating too hard,' she said thickly, blinking.

'Then take a break. Take me to task while you drink your tea.'

She looked up at him. 'For what, exactly?'

'Continue with the lecture you gave me last night.'

'It doesn't seem important any more,' she muttered, and gulped some tea.

'You were annoyed because I didn't say it was my grandmother's birthday,' he prompted, perching on a corner of the desk.

'That was part of it. I would have liked to give her something more inspired than mere chocolates.'

'Are you still angry?'

'Not after meeting your grandmother. Who could be? And we've already cleared up the identity of the beautiful Nicola—who still carries a torch for you, by the way.'

His jaw tightened. 'You're imagining things. We parted by mutual consent.'

'You mean you ran a mile when she mentioned marriage!' she retorted.

Ewen's bloodshot eyes glittered dangerously. 'We merely agreed to disagree on the subject. Like you, Nicola's hooked on getting married. To someone else these days, as it happens—a nice, nine-to-five kind of guy who'll make her a lot happier than I ever did.'

'You obviously keep up with her, then.'

He shrugged. 'Her sister married my cousin. I can't fail to keep up.'

'I like her,' said Rosanna.

'Oddly enough, so do I.' Ewen looked at her challengingly. 'Right. Now we've disposed of Nicola, let's talk about what happened in the lift.'

Rosanna's heart gave a thud against her shirt. 'I'm not angry about that,' she said carefully. 'It was my fault, anyway.'

His eyebrows shot up to his hair. '*Your* fault!'

She nodded glumly. 'I was hysterical, you comforted me, and the inevitable happened.' She managed a smile. 'A good thing the power came back just then.'

Ewen's eyes locked with hers. 'What would have happened if it hadn't?'

'I refuse to think about that.'

'Whereas I can't stop thinking about it.'

'If I'm honest neither can I, but for a different reason.' Her eyes glittered. 'You're a very practised lover, Ewen Fraser. And after seeing you in action yesterday it's easy to see how you acquired such skill.'

His jaw clenched. 'What happened between you and me, Rosanna, owed nothing to skill. It was sheer magic.'

'I bet you say that to all the girls,' she said cuttingly.

'Actually I don't. Or didn't, if we're to use the correct tense.' Ewen moved closer. 'Since meeting you, Rosanna, I've had no contact with other women of any kind. It's the honest truth. Do you believe me?'

She frowned, secretly shaken to find she really did believe him. 'It doesn't really matter whether I do or not, does it? I'm committed to someone else. As you said, I'm the marrying kind. Which makes my behaviour a lot worse than yours. I'm sorry I was so—so shameless in the lift yesterday. I've never behaved like that before in my life.'

'Never?' Ewen raised a mocking eyebrow and stood up. 'Don't worry, it won't happen again unless—'

'Unless what?' she demanded.

'Unless we get stuck in a lift again, I suppose,' he said negligently. 'In the meantime,

Rosanna, you're in no danger. My brute instincts are safe under lock and key once more.'

Over the next few days Rosanna began to doubt they'd ever get back to their previous, effortless rapport. Admittedly there'd always been an undercurrent beneath the friendly surface, a frisson that added an extra dimension to their working relationship. But these days the air literally crackled with tension during their brief dealings together. It was a relief when Ewen went out to lunch with his agent one day the following week. Rosanna was glad to be free of his brooding presence, which disturbed her even when he was shut away upstairs in his study. She was left in peace all day. There was no sign of Ewen by the time she was ready to go. Some lunch, she thought huffily, and went home on the stroke of six for once.

Next morning Rosanna arrived early. And wished she hadn't. As she turned into the mews she caught a glimpse of Ewen embracing a woman who got into a taxi as Rosanna dodged out of sight and stayed there, heart pounding, until the coast was clear. This was ridiculous, she told herself bitterly, trying to calm down. Ewen Fraser was a virile male who attracted women like flies. His sex life was nothing to do with Rosanna Carey. To accustom herself to this line of thinking she went for a walk, fighting the searing jealousy she had no right to. Something, it was obvious, had to be done about it. The moment Ewen's first draft was finished she was off to Boston.

When she could face going back to the house Rosanna apologised to Ewen for her late arrival, but to her surprise Ewen greeted her with something like his old, friendly manner. A night spent in feminine company had obviously done wonders for his frame of mind, she thought bitterly. Rosanna soon found she had cause to be grateful to the lady. Diplomatic relations, it seemed, had been resumed.

But as the day wore on she recognised a faint but definite withdrawal on Ewen's part, as though he'd drawn a demarcation line between them. Now he had another woman, it seemed, things would be different. Rosanna was proved right. In the period that followed Ewen worked harder than ever before, ate his lunch at his desk, and no longer asked her to stay for a drink some evenings when it was time to go home. Which was all to the good, Rosanna told herself firmly. She'd been in danger of getting too close to Ewen Fraser. Her future lay with David. Not, she thought morosely, that Ewen had ever professed interest in her future. He'd made it plain he just wanted a brief, physical love affair in the present. And even that stemmed from her resemblance to Rose.

The Careys duly returned from Australia, full of their trip, and eager for news of Rosanna's work for Ewen Fraser, and after spending a few days in Ealing with them Rosanna moved back into the flat with Louise, the reluctant Paula having at last found somewhere else to live.

After a couple of weeks of almost constant rain July turned hot and sunny, and Rosanna soon found the confines of the basement flat claustrophobic and stuffy. Ewen's house enjoyed the luxury of air-conditioning, and at the height of the sudden heatwave Rosanna found it an effort to leave each evening. She was sleeping badly, and life with the bouncy Louise was proving less easy to cope with after a break away from it. She was getting old before her time, her friend said crossly.

The melancholy truth, Rosanna admitted bleakly, was that these days she just didn't seem to belong anywhere. She'd flown the Ealing nest long ago, but now she also seemed to have grown out of the life once enjoyed to the full with Louise. It was just a phase, she assured herself. She just needed a holiday in Boston.

'You look very pale,' said Ewen, one Friday night.

'It's the heat.' Rosanna smiled. 'The flat's stuffy in this weather. It's shrunk in some mysterious way during my time away from it.'

'You're obviously not sleeping well.'

'The heat again. I yearn for fresh air.' She sighed. 'My ambition is to live in the country one day.' She stacked the day's output neatly, ready for Ewen to read, then looked up to find him watching her.

'What are you doing this weekend?' he asked casually.

Rosanna's heart missed a beat. 'Nothing much. Chores and shopping tomorrow. Sunday lunch with my parents, that kind of thing.'

'If you yearn for the country skip the chores and come for a drive tomorrow instead.' Ewen looked at her squarely. 'I'll bring you back any time you say.'

His lady not available? thought Rosanna.

'It was just a thought,' he said stiffly. 'Or are you afraid your doctor would object?'

'On the contrary, he'd be glad I was escaping this heat.' Rosanna shrugged. 'If you want the truth I was wondering why you were at a loose end tomorrow.'

Ewen looked blank. 'I'm not. No more than any other weekend. I usually work right through. But it's so hot I fancy a day off.'

'Isn't your friend free to go with you?'

'My friend,' he repeated, eyes narrowed. 'Who do you mean, Rosanna?'

'I saw someone leaving early one morning a few weeks ago, just as I arrived,' she said reluctantly.

Ewen stared at her, then smiled slowly in a way which raised Rosanna's hackles. 'You were right. It *was* a friend. Harriet Wallace, my editor, to be exact. She lives nearby so she called round on her way in to work to show me the artwork for the cover.' His eyes bored into hers. 'But naturally my famed reputation convinced you she stayed the night with me. If she did her husband would have something to say about it, believe me.'

Rosanna did believe him, much to her embarrassment. 'I apologise,' she said stiffly. 'Your private life is absolutely none of my concern.'

'As I told you before, Rosanna,' he said with quiet emphasis, 'since I met you I haven't been out—or in—with any woman. The situation remains unchanged. In every way.'

Rosanna looked at him in silence for a moment, then gave him an awkward little smile. 'If the offer still stands I really would love a trip to the country tomorrow.'

Ewen's answering smile was the first really genuine one he'd favoured her with in quite a while. 'Good. In that case, let's make an early start, get out of town while it's relatively quiet.'

'Thank you. I'd like that.'

'I'll come for you at nine, then. Where's this flat of yours?' He eyed her quizzically. 'Or would you rather I didn't pick you up there?'

'Of course not,' she said quickly, and gave him the address. Louise was away for the weekend, so the outing with Ewen would go unremarked upon anyway, but she saw no reason to tell him that.

'Are you in a rush to get home, or would you like a drink?' asked Ewen, surprising her even more.

'No, and yes, please, in that order,' she said quickly, deeply relieved that they were back on a friendly footing again. And with the news that the mystery blonde was not Nicola Blake, as she'd suspected, her spirits rose even further. For the first time since the fateful Sunday of the storm they sat talking over the progress of the novel with something like their original ease in each other's company.

'By the end of next month I should be finished,' said Ewen, and raised his glass of beer in toast. 'My editor was impressed. Due to your help I'm much further along than I believed possible at this stage.'

'Good,' said Rosanna with satisfaction. 'I'm glad the labourer was worthy of the hire.'

'The description doesn't suit you much, Rosanna.' He smiled, leaning back on the sofa opposite her, his long legs stretched out in front of him. 'Why are you looking at me like that?'

'As usual your hair needs cutting,' she said frankly, and he let out a crack of laughter.

'You sound like my mother.'

'Good. I like your mother.'

Ewen smiled. 'She liked you, too. You made a good impression on both my parents.'

'It was mutual. I liked your grandmother, too.' But thoughts of the birthday party led to memories of what happened afterwards, and Rosanna downed the last of her drink and stood up. 'That was lovely, but I must be on my way. The taxi will be here any minute.'

'Anywhere special you'd like to go tomorrow?' he asked.

'As long as it's leafy and green and cool I'll be happy,' she said cheerfully, and collected her belongings as the doorbell rang. 'I'm away. Thanks for the drink.'

'I'll see you in the morning, then. Nine sharp for the magical mystery tour,' said Ewen, walking to the door with her.

Rosanna smiled at him, and went out into the breathless, hot evening feeling a lot happier than of late. David, she decided without guilt, could spare her one harmless drive into the country.

Rosanna woke early next morning after the first good night's sleep she'd had for weeks. And her reflection in the bathroom mirror looked very different from the hurried, harassed creature who normally rushed past it in the mornings.

The day was already hot, and instead of jeans Rosanna decided on the rose-printed blue skirt with a sleeveless cream silk shirt, and carried a linen jacket just in case the weather decided to change. When her bell rang shortly before nine she locked up, then ran upstairs to the front door, where Ewen was waiting for her, in familiar pale khakis and a thin yellow shirt.

'Good morning,' he said, eyeing her. 'You look a lot different from the girl who went home last night.'

'Sleep is the best beauty aid there is,' she told him blithely as they hurried to the space Ewen had found for the Morgan. 'I'm amazed you left her here all alone,' she teased.

'It wasn't easy!' Ewen patted the gleaming dark green bonnet lovingly, then got in the car. 'Right, then. Let's go. Did you bring a scarf?'

She shook her head. 'I want the wind in my hair.'

The trip began with the inevitable drive along a motorway, and after an hour or so of heading west Ewen told her they were making for deepest Gloucestershire. Content to let Ewen conduct her on this mystery trip he'd promised, Rosanna sat back in her seat and prepared to enjoy the cloudless day and her escape from the city.

'Do you want the hood up?' shouted Ewen, eyeing her streaming hair, but Rosanna shook her head.

'This is wonderful,' she assured him, though she was glad, eventually, when Ewen left the motorway. They passed through villages alive with Saturday bustle, and eventually took a turning down a road so narrow, trees mingled their branches overhead, forming a shady green tunnel for a while until the trees on one side gave way to a stone wall which lined the road as far as the eye could see.

'Cooler now?' asked Ewen.

Rosanna nodded blissfully. 'Am I allowed to ask where we are yet?'

'On the outskirts of Long Ashley, but we don't go as far as the village itself. In fact we've arrived.' Ewen slowed the car and turned through gates which stood open at a break in the wall, then parked outside a solid stone cottage which had obviously once been the gatehouse of some large residence. There was a small garden in the front, fragrant with rose and lavender, and she gazed at the house in silence for a moment.

'Is this our destination?' she asked Ewen warily. 'Are you springing me on another un-suspecting relative?'

'In a way, yes.' He got out and came round the car to offer Rosanna his hand, smiling down into her suspicious face.

'Who lives here, then?' she demanded, sliding out of the car.

'I do. At weekends sometimes, or when the city gets too much. You were in need of fresh country air, so I thought you'd like to see my retreat.'

Rosanna eyed the house with respect. 'Your books must sell very well!'

'I didn't buy the cottage, the Brigadier left it to me. He spent the last few years of his life here.' Ewen opened the small iron gate and ushered her through it. 'Come and explore.'

Rosanna followed him along the short, gravelled path, eyeing the cottage covetously. Ewen unlocked the front door on a narrow hall with walls painted pale gold, high Victorian covings and a dado rail picked out in white. Ewen took her on a brief tour of small, high-ceilinged rooms with large bay windows to give the illusion of space. Unlike Ewen's uncluttered flat the house was filled with old pine furniture, comfortable sofas, shelves filled with blue and white porcelain, framed photographs on tables, and pictures grouped together on every available inch of wall space.

'There must have been a good fairy at your christening, Ewen Fraser,' said Rosanna with an envious sigh. 'This is just lovely. Is it your taste, or Harry's?'

'A blend of both. This is one of five lodges dotted round the estate of a big country house. These days the house is a conference centre, and all the cottages are privately owned.' Ewen led the way through a small, functional kitchen to a conservatory which wrapped around the back of the house. 'My first priorities were a new bed, and modernising the bathroom and kitchen. This was finished only recently.'

Rosanna was consumed with envy as she gazed through the conservatory windows at Ewen's back garden. Colourful herbaceous borders surrounded a small lawn shaded by a tall hedge, where a central iron gate opened on a large vegetable garden beyond.

Ewen grinned at the look on her face. 'Before you ask, a man from the village does the gardening. Bob's plot is much smaller, so he grows what he likes here, and gives me a few vegetables now and then. I pay him to see to the rest, and his daughter comes in to clean once a week to top up her pocket money. The arrangement works very well.'

Rosanna was impressed as they walked round the garden. 'So this is where the broad beans came from. No wonder they tasted so good.'

'Let's have some coffee, and you can tell me how you'd like to spend the rest of the day.' Ewen looked down at her as they strolled back to the house. 'Or are you going out to-night? Do you need to be back early?'

'No.' Far from leaving early, Rosanna wanted to stay in this enchanted place as long as possible.

They took their coffee into the conservatory, where Rosanna relaxed in a long wicker chaise with the newspaper Ewen handed her. Using it as a shield, she studied Ewen's absorbed, clever face covertly, and made a vow. No more days like this. It was too unsettling. Ewen's cottage was her dream of a country home made reality. Whereas her future would inevitably involve a town with a hospital prestigious enough to offer David Norton the type of post he was working towards.

'The pub in the village does a decent meal,' said Ewen, breaking into her thoughts. 'Fancy a stroll?'

'Sounds good,' said Rosanna, and swung her feet to the ground, smiling brightly. 'I'll just run upstairs and tidy up first, please.'

'Don't take too long,' he warned. 'The Rose and Crown gets packed on Saturdays.'

Upstairs Rosanna peeped into a spare room empty except for a chair and a battered desk, but the dominant feature in the master bed-room was a large bed with a carved headboard. The tall bay window was hung with dark blue curtains looped back with thick white ropes, and a plain, wood-framed mirror surmounted a solid pine table where Rose smiled her sweet, seductive smile from a silver frame.

Rosanna gazed for a moment, stung by a sudden pang of pure jealousy, then she gave a wry smile of apology to the photograph and went into the small bathroom, where Ewen's taste was very much in evidence. The exterior of a reclaimed cast-iron hip bath had been painted terracotta to match the walls, with a white venetian blind on the tall window, and every inch of free space lined with books.

'I like your bathroom,' she said, when she rejoined Ewen downstairs.

'Did you look in the bedroom?'

'From the doorway, yes. I saw Rose.'

Ewen nodded. 'She's always lived here. Which is why I wouldn't let you have the photograph.'

'Did you come here much when your uncle was alive?' Rosanna asked as they left the house.

'As often as he'd put up with me. I've always loved the place. The old boy did most of the gardening himself in those days. I was expected to help. And wash up and make my bed and keep myself scrubbed as well. No slovenliness for the Brigadier.'

Rosanna smiled. 'My grandmother was the same. She always faced the day fully made up, and hair perfect.'

Ewen glanced at her as they strolled along the quiet road in the hot noon sunshine. 'He never stopped loving her. Do you think she felt the same?'

'Of course she did,' said Rosanna without hesitation. 'Otherwise why tell me the gold rose was her most treasured possession? Besides,' she added, 'my mother's name is Henrietta.'

Ewen stopped dead, looking at her. 'She named her only child after him?'

'I didn't realise that until I found out about Harry. But it's obvious, now. My grandfather never knew Rose had met someone else, so he wouldn't have attached any significance to the name,' she added as they resumed walking.

The Rose and Crown was a picturesque place, and already half full. They found a small table in a corner near a window, and drank half pints of shandy, and ate vast slices of grilled ham with tomatoes and mushrooms, and in Ewen's case two fried eggs.

'*Two* eggs,' said Rosanna, laughing.

'Why not?' he said, unmoved. 'I'll run an extra mile or two tomorrow.'

'On a day like this we should be eating nice healthy salads,' she said, munching ecstatically. 'Not that this isn't wonderful.'

'You can have salad for supper.'

So she was staying for supper, thought Rosanna.

'How would you like to spend the afternoon?' asked Ewen.

'Just sitting in your heavenly back garden.'

'You could do some hoeing if you like,' he offered with a grin.

'No way!' Rosanna smiled cajolingly. 'I hoped you'd take that wicker chaise out on the lawn for me. I'd like to get some sun.'

Ewen resumed his lunch. 'Good idea. I'll join you.'

CHAPTER EIGHT

THE small garden was completely secluded behind its neatly clipped hedges, with only the rustling of the leaves in a pair of apple trees to break the silence. It was an idyllic way to spend a hot Saturday afternoon, thought Rosanna.

'Why the sigh?' asked Ewen.

'I was just thinking how perfect your life is,' she told him bluntly.

He frowned. 'Perfect?'

She nodded 'Everything seems to fall in your lap. You write bestsellers, own *two* houses, the Morgan—'

'Hey! Hold on.' He held up a hand. 'It's one bestseller, and two previous, reasonably successful books written while I was working full-time as a journalist. And working damned hard, too. And not so long ago my London home was a humdrum flat in Wandsworth. I moved into the Chelsea house only recently.'

Ewen paused, slanting a look at her. 'My life's not entirely perfect, Rosanna. I live in both places alone.'

'Only by choice,' she retorted.

'True,' he conceded. 'The brief experiment with Nicola taught me a salutary lesson.'

To her intense annoyance Rosanna felt a pang of jealousy at the thought of Ewen sharing his life with Nicola, or any other woman. 'Did she like this place?' she asked.

'I never brought her here,' he said shortly. 'The only one I share the cottage with is Rose.'

Rosanna nodded resignedly. 'As I've said before, Ewen Fraser, you're in love with a ghost.'

'More convenient that way,' he said blandly. 'She doesn't object when I work far into the night, or feel too tired to go out on the town.'

With an effort Rosanna managed to hold her tongue rather than disrupt the afternoon with an argument.

After a while Ewen got up. 'You just lie there and soak up the sun. I've got a few telephone calls to make.'

Rosanna settled down obediently, only too glad to do as he said, and woke from a sound sleep later to find Ewen tickling her nose with a blade of grass.

'I was afraid you'd burn,' he said, smiling.

Rosanna sat up, pushing her hair back, her face warm from more than the sun. 'Have I been asleep long? What time is it?'

'Just after six, Tea, or a drink?'

'Drink, please. Something long, cold and non-alcoholic.' Rosanna yawned, then pulled a face. 'Sorry to be so rude. I gave up afternoon naps when I was a baby.'

'The slave-driver you work for has obviously worn you out!'

'That must be it,' she agreed lightly, and got up. 'I need some repairs.'

'I'll have your drink waiting when you come down.'

When Rosanna's hair was brushed and her face touched up a little she heard voices and went back downstairs to find a pretty, fair-haired teenager talking to Ewen in the kitchen. The girl wore skin-tight jeans and a clinging knit top, and she was smiling up at Ewen with a starry look in her heavily painted eyes.

'Ah, Rosanna,' he said quickly, and came towards her, putting an arm round her waist. 'Meet Sally Todd. She keeps the place tidy for me.'

'Hello, Sally, I'm Rosanna Carey. Nice to meet you.' She kept her face straight with effort as Ewen's arm tightened possessively.

The girl was openly taken aback at the sight of Rosanna. After a moment she forced a smile. 'Hello—sorry, but you're just like—'

'The photograph upstairs,' said Rosanna resignedly.

The girl nodded her mop of tousled blonde curls. 'I'm ever so fond of it. I dust it when I come in to clean. You're the image of the lady.'

'Miss Carey's her granddaughter,' explained Ewen.

'Oh, right.' Sally lost interest. 'My mum thought you'd like a cake for your tea, Mr Fraser, and Dad sent the tomatoes from our greenhouse. He said to take what vegetables you want when you go back. I didn't know you had visitors,' said the girl awkwardly. 'I'd better be going, then.'

'Thanks for coming, Sally. And thank your mother and father for me,' said Ewen, releasing Rosanna to see the girl out.

'Goodbye, Sally,' said Rosanna warmly.

When Ewen rejoined her she wagged a finger at him. 'So that's why you brought me down here today—as your cover again,' she accused, laughing. 'Are you always in such constant danger from my sex, Ewen Fraser?'

'Of course not!' he said, grinning reluctantly. 'But I'm damned glad you were here. Sally usually cleans the place on a Saturday, so I rang her father to tell her not to bother this week. But she came bearing gifts instead.'

Rosanna shook her head at him. 'Take my advice, Ewen Fraser. Tread carefully with that pretty little gift horse. Sally's got an outsize crush on you.'

'I'd have to be blind not to notice it,' he said ruefully. 'That's why I put on the possessive act when you appeared.'

'Very effective it was, too. It damped poor Sally down like a cold shower. And my famed likeness to Rose up there added the finishing touch. It's probably put her off you completely.'

'Pity,' said Ewen, investigating the contents of the tin. 'Lusting maidens work wonders for the male ego. Though it's a shame she doesn't do something with that hair, poor kid.'

'You poor, unsuspecting male!' Rosanna hooted with laughter. 'It took her hours to get it like that.'

'You're not serious?' He grinned. 'Come on. I suggest we drink this in the conservatory. The insect population will be out in full force in the garden by this time.'

Rosanna was halfway through her tall glass of grape juice when the truth suddenly made its presence felt. There was no blinding flash of revelation. Just a sudden removal of the blinkers she'd fought so hard to keep in place. For years she'd had tunnel vision about men, never diverted from her love for David, which was a safe, solid emotion she was very comfortable with. But there was no use trying to kid herself any longer. She was *in* love with Ewen Fraser, a dangerous, physical fire of an emotion ready at any time to blaze out of control. She stole a look at his face as she came to terms with the truth, then turned her eyes back to the garden. Fire, she reminded herself, soon died out without fuel to feed on. And this fire would have to. She would make it die.

'You're very quiet,' said Ewen eventually. He sat with his back to the light, his face hidden in the lengthening shadows.

'I was savouring the peace before going back to the city.'

'Let's wait until it's dark and a lot cooler than this before we do. Don't worry,' he added. 'I'll put the hood up.'

After Rosanna's moment of self-revelation in the conservatory her first reaction was to leave precipitately, to make some excuse and ask Ewen to drive her home at once. But this would never happen again, she argued with herself. And it was a bittersweet experience to help Ewen with their simple meal, then share it with him at the round table in his tiny dining room. They talked easily together, with no hint of the recent hostility between them, but

Rosanna ate very little, blaming her mammoth lunch for her lack of appetite, and Ewen ate very little more than she did. For the same reason, he told her.

As they talked their eyes met constantly and slid away, the electricity in the air between them mounting as the light faded, and the candles flickered now and then in the slight, scented breeze which drifted through the open windows.

'You like my country cottage, then?' asked Ewen huskily.

Rosanna sighed. 'It's lovely. I envy you.' She sought for something unemotional to say. 'Are you going to furnish the spare room upstairs as another bedroom some time?'

He shook his head, smiling crookedly. 'Didn't you wonder a little, at the time, how I managed to get a second computer installed in the mews house so rapidly?'

Her eyes widened. 'Oh, I *see*—it was here! On that desk upstairs. You had it sent up.'

'Bob Todd brought it in his van.'

'So why didn't you tell me?'

'Normally I do most of my writing down here. I bought a computer for the Chelsea house only recently.'

'Then what made you start working on your book in London instead?'

Ewen's eyes, gold-flecked and gleaming in the candlelight, locked with hers. 'Can't you think of a reason, Rosanna?'

She could, but it was so far-fetched she hadn't the nerve to put it into words. 'You needed to be more handy for your editor, or for more research material?'

'No. I was determined to persuade you to work with me.'

Rosanna's eyes narrowed. 'And at the same time provide you with a living, breathing incarnation of Rose Norman right before your eyes. A novel way of doing research,' she said without inflection.

He shook his head. 'It was nothing to do with research. Or Rose. Only you. I made that plain, right from the beginning, Rosanna. I even wrote to you on the subject.'

'So you did,' she murmured, heat rising in her cheeks.

'But you faxed me, telling me to stop.' His mouth twisted. 'A very effective way of dampening my ardour.'

'It was meant to be.'

They looked at each other in silence in the shadowy room.

'This was a mistake today,' she said at last, and he nodded slowly.

'I know. But you looked so tired and pale and unhappy last night. I'd meant to keep this place a secret. I never had any intention of bringing you here.' He smiled wryly. 'One ghost is enough for any man.'

'I'm not a ghost, Ewen.'

'You'll haunt the place just the same.' He jerked his head towards the garden. 'Out there in the sun, in here sharing a meal. Just being here. Dammit, Rosanna, you know I want you. Since that night in the lift I've fought like hell to keep my distance. The morning after I was all set to give you your marching orders. Tell you I could only take so much. But my hangover got in the way. And by the time I was over it there you were, working away at the computer, and it was too late.'

She let out a deep, shaky breath. 'I nearly didn't come that day. I dreaded facing you again, after the way I behaved—'

'The way *you* behaved!' He stared at her blankly. 'I was the one who took advantage of the situation, Rosanna.'

'No, you didn't. I was equally to blame.' Her eyes fell. 'I really am claustrophobic, but once you started making love to me I forgot all about it. It was a revelation. I never dreamed...'

The candles guttered and went out, but neither of them moved. They both sat motionless in the semi-darkness, her words hanging in the air between them. At last Ewen got slowly to his feet, came round the table, and drew her up into his arms. He held her in a loose embrace, his cheek on her hair, and she leaned against him, unresisting.

'It's time I drove you home,' he whispered, and she nodded, and Ewen sighed heavily and put her away from him a little, his smile more crooked than ever as he linked his hands at the back of her waist. 'No storm tonight.'

I wish there were, she thought, then caught his eye and knew he'd read her mind.

'Would you stay if there were?' he asked.

Rosanna considered lying, but decided against it. 'I would want to,' she said honestly, and he pulled her close, rubbing his cheek against hers.

'Why did you come today?'

'Because I wanted to. But I didn't know you were going to bring me to a place like this.' Suddenly her eyes brimmed over, and she buried her face in his shirt. 'I wish you hadn't!'

He turned her face up to his with an inexorable finger. 'But you told me you wanted to live in the country one day. Has this place changed your mind?'

'No. Quite the reverse. I didn't tell you the rest, how I wanted a cottage and a garden, with children and dogs. Pretty funny, isn't it? The closest I'll get to children for years is teaching them.' She sniffed inelegantly, and knuckled her tears away. 'Sorry. I didn't mean to cry all over you, Ewen. Time we went back to the real world.'

His eyes glittered with a look which made her heart pound, but instead of kissing her he mopped her face prosaically with her napkin. 'I suppose you're right, Rosanna Carey. Back to the big city, then.'

'First we tidy up.' Rosanna gave him a determined smile, and began clearing away the remains of the meal as he switched on some of the lamps. 'What shall I do with the wine? Neither of us drank much.'

'Throw it away. And the leftovers. But I'd better take the tomatoes and the cake back with me. I'd hate to offend the family Todd.'

They worked rapidly together, but in her haste to finish washing up Rosanna grasped the razor-sharp paring knife by the blade. 'Oops,' she said faintly. 'I've cut myself.'

Ewen turned on the cold tap and held her hand under it. 'It looks deep,' he said, frowning. 'I hope I've got some plasters somewhere— Rosanna!' He seized her in his arms as she began to crumple.

Ewen carried her to the sofa, and she swung her feet to the ground and put her head between her knees while he searched for some plasters. He came back with one and some antiseptic, and knelt beside her to dress the cut.

'I forgot to mention,' she croaked, 'that I'm not only claustrophobic, I can't stand the sight of blood.'

'Some doctor's wife you're going to be!' he said grimly, wiping the perspiration from her forehead. 'How do you feel?'

'I'm always fine once the blood's gone.' She sat up with care. 'See? Good as new.'

'You're a bit pale.'

'So are you.'

They eyed each other in a silence which grew so prolonged she smiled shakily at last, then felt her heart leap as Ewen's eyes blazed with such molten heat that her blood thundered in her veins in response; then she was in his arms, and he was kissing her with a starving desperation she responded to in kind, all her shaky defences knocked flat.

'I wasn't going to do this,' he panted against her mouth.

'I know,' she gasped, and pulled him closer, her lips parting in such open invitation, Ewen's scruples were routed.

They fell full-length together on the sofa in a tangle of arms and legs, kissing wildly as though their lives depended on the contact of mouth and hands and bodies that strained together as though neither could exist in separation.

'Stay with me tonight!' said Ewen hoarsely, and she nodded feverishly, and he brought his mouth down hard on hers. She gasped and clutched him closer, her mouth opening to his tongue as she shook in the throes of a desire so intense she could hardly bear it, glad when Ewen suddenly pulled her to her feet and hurried her towards the stairs. Arms round each other, kissing wildly all the way, their progress upward was so erratic they stumbled, laughing breathlessly, unwilling to separate for even the short distance to the landing. But when they reached his room Ewen whispered, 'One second,' went inside, and came back almost at once, to pick her up, carry her into the moonlit room and lay her on his bed.

'No Rose,' she whispered, smiling luminously as she stretched up her arms.

Ewen came down to her, holding her close. 'She was Harry's girl. The only woman *I* want is you. Warm, breathing, living Rosanna. And I want you so much I don't think I can be gentle—'

CHAPTER NINE

ROSANNA surrendered herself without reserve, her arousal heightened by the unsteadiness of Ewen's hands as he undressed her. Then they were naked together at last, with no barriers of clothes, or ghosts from the past. Or from the present. There was nothing in the world other than the sensations coursing through her body as Ewen caressed every part of her into feverish response, until she was breathless and trembling, her hands urgent with caresses of their own. Ewen's kisses were less frenzied now, slow, deep and hot, like honeyed fire on her mouth and throat, on the breasts which tautened at his touch. Then his head moved lower and his kisses moved to hitherto uncharted territory. The breath cut through her lungs in agonising gasps as his fingers wrought dark magic, and sunbursts of light showered behind her tightly closed eyelids. His kisses slid up her trembling thighs then his mouth

189

was on hers again, and his hands were beneath her hips, and they gave a simultaneous, shuddering sigh as their bodies joined.

Ewen began to move involuntarily, and Rosanna held him close and moved with him in a rhythm which grew to a frenzied crescendo as he took her to the very brink of ecstasy at last, held her there for an endless, throbbing moment, then fell with her over the edge into fulfilment so intense, sleep overcame Rosanna almost instantly.

She woke at some point to find Ewen drawing the covers over them before taking her back into his warm, already familiar embrace, then she sank back, unresisting, into a sleep so deep she thought she was dreaming when she felt caressing, cajoling fingers on her skin, and a mouth which pressed warm, drugging kisses against her neck and shoulders. She gave a low, dreamy little sound of contentment and stretched luxuriously, letting the tide of sensation lap over her, until she was fully awake and Ewen's mouth was on hers, and it was all happening again, slower now, with long-drawn-out attention paid to every step of the way. Rosanna grew bolder in the dark cocoon of warmth beneath the covers. Her questing touch brought Ewen to breaking point with deeply gratifying speed, and he rolled her beneath him, captured her hands and held them wide, his knee nudging her thighs apart as he kissed her fiercely and took possession of her once more.

When Rosanna woke next it was daylight, and she was alone in the wildly untidy bed. She straightened the covers hastily and pulled them up to her chin, pushing the hair out of her eyes as Ewen backed through the door with a laden tray.

He put it down carefully on the bedside table, then grinned at her broadly as he bowed and handed her a snapdragon.

'Good morning. I thought you'd prefer this to a rose.'

'Good morning,' she said breathlessly, feeling absurdly shy. 'Thank you. Have you been out in the garden like that?' She eyed his towelling robe, which ended halfway down his thighs.

'No one to see,' he said unrepentantly. 'Coffee?'

'Yes, please.'

He filled a cup and handed it to her. 'I didn't bother to get dressed.' He leaned a hand either side of her on the bed, smiling down into her eyes. 'I thought I'd get back in here with you for breakfast.'

Rosanna looked away, and felt him stiffen.

'Somehow I don't think you care for the idea.' Ewen straightened and poured himself some coffee, then sat on the edge of the bed, pointedly keeping his distance. 'You're obviously not a morning person, Rosanna Carey.'

'True,' she said, and gulped some coffee. 'I'm also very untidy, I haven't brushed my teeth, and I'd like a bath.'

'By the time you've done all that the toast will be greasy and the coffee cold,' he pointed out.

'I'm not hungry,' she muttered.

'All right, Rosanna,' he said wearily. 'I can take a hint. I'll top up your coffee then take my unwanted breakfast—and myself—downstairs.'

'Thank you.' She looked up at him in appeal. 'Could we leave soon, please?'

His eyes narrowed to the slanting gleam which always made her apprehensive. 'Of course. What time do you have to be back?'

'I'm due at my parents' house at twelve.'

'Right,' he said curtly. 'We'll leave about ten. Take your time over your bath.'

When Ewen had gone Rosanna laid her head on her drawn-up knees and gave way to a few bitter, unrelieving tears, then threw back the covers, picked up her clothes and shut herself in the bathroom. There was only one toothbrush in sight, but just this once Ewen would have to let her use it. After a rapid but blessedly hot bath she felt a little better, but there was nothing she could do about the creases in her skirt and blouse, which lay in a crumpled heap where Ewen had thrown them on the floor. Heat rushed all over her at the thought of it, and it took her a moment or two to recover before she went downstairs to find her handbag to complete the tidying-up process.

Ewen was in the garden, scattering the uneaten toast for the birds. The day was cloudier, with a cool breeze, and he was shivering a little as he came back in. 'You were quick,' he said briskly. 'I'll have a bath myself before we go. Make some more coffee if you want.'

'Thank you,' said Rosanna, thoroughly miserable by this time.

While Ewen was upstairs she searched in her handbag for lipstick, combed her hair, then she put on the linen jacket and buttoned it up over the creased silk shirt. When he came back she was sitting in the conservatory with a cup of fresh coffee, looking at one of the previous day's newspapers.

'There's more coffee in the pot,' she offered.

'Good,' he said brusquely, and went off to fetch it, looking a lot better than she did, thought Rosanna resentfully. He was wearing a clean blue shirt and linen trousers, and had shaved and taken some time to subdue his unruly hair. It was his house, of course. He had everything to hand. But it put her at a disadvantage to feel grubby and rumpled and less than her best.

'So,' said Ewen, sitting down beside her. 'What now, Rosanna?'

She made no pretence of misunderstanding. 'Ewen, last night was wonderful, enchanted, like nothing that's ever happened to me before—'

'By which,' he interrupted bitingly, 'I take it you don't intend it to happen again.' He turned to look at her, his eyes narrowed dangerously. 'Are you telling me it was just a one-night stand?'

'Please don't cheapen it, Ewen,' she begged. 'I'm sorry. It was my fault—'

'No, it damn well wasn't your fault,' he snapped. 'It was mutual, Rosanna.' He stared out into the garden, his face grim. 'I write too much fiction, I suppose, a devotee of the happy ending syndrome. I had this far-fetched idea that after last night you'd admit that we're meant for each other. That we belong.'

'Even if I did admit it, I can't do anything about it,' she said, anguished. She turned reddened, tear-wet eyes on him. 'When you asked me down here did you intend it to happen?'

Ewen said nothing for a moment, then he turned to look at her, his mouth twisting as he saw her unshed tears. 'I didn't intend it. But I suppose some secret part of me hoped it would. I'm human—and male.' His eyes hardened. 'But you fell in love with the cottage, not me. I was mad to ask you to stay on for supper.'

'You only asked,' she pointed out. 'I could have said no.'

'Then why the hell didn't you?'

'I wish I had now,' she said with passion.

'Why?' He reached out a hand and took hers, his fingers tightening cruelly.

Rosanna flinched. 'Because then last night would never have happened. But it did. And now I've got to try and forget it. Lord knows how, but I must. I've promised to marry David. I've never been unfaithful to him before—' She breathed in sharply. 'Ewen, please! You're hurting me.'

He flung her hand away and stared blindly at the garden. 'What would you say if I asked you to marry me instead?' he said at last, as though the words were forced out of him.

'*What?* Rosanna glared at him, incensed. 'After all you've said about marriage? It would serve you right if I said yes. Not that I would even if you were serious. I couldn't hurt David like that.'

'You're ready to hurt *me*,' he said bitterly.

'I don't *want* to,' she said in desperation. 'But, Ewen, we haven't known each other long. If it hadn't been for Rose, and Harry, we wouldn't know each other as well as we do. But my future lies with David. He's been working so hard for years, just to make it possible for us to marry. I can't throw all that up in exchange for a love affair with you. Much as I—' She stopped dead.

After a taut, pregnant silence Ewen asked silkily, 'What were you going to say, Rosanna?'

'Much as I like you,' she went on doggedly, 'I love David. I've behaved appallingly. I freely admit it. I should never have come here yesterday—nor agreed to work for you in the first place.'

'So why did you?' he said inexorably.

She shrugged, a wry smile at the corners of her mouth. 'You know why. That's what you always say to me.'

'But I don't know why,' he said through his teeth. 'Explain.'

Because I'm in love with you, she thought despairingly. 'Because of Rose and Harry,' she said aloud. 'I suppose I felt—involved.'

'And now you're going to let history repeat itself.' Ewen got up suddenly and pulled her up into his arms. 'You and I *could* have a happy ending, Rosanna. You're not Rose, giving up the man she loved for the wounded war hero. And I'm not Harry, either, the gentleman prepared to take no for an answer.'

'Please don't, Ewen!' Tears gathered in Rosanna's eyes, and slid down her cheeks. 'You want what happened last night. I want it, too. But you know it wouldn't last. My relationship with David is different, the durable kind—'

'And do you tremble for him like this?' said Ewen hoarsely, and licked away the tears on her cheeks. His mouth found hers, one hand undoing her jacket to caress her, and she stiffened and tried to push him away, but he held her close, kissing her with an angry desperation she responded to helplessly. Neither of them noticed the girl standing in the kitchen doorway until her loud cough brought them back to earth.

'I saw the car was still here,' said Sally, darting a hostile look at Rosanna. 'I thought you'd like the Sunday papers.'

'Hello, Sally,' said Ewen with forced cheerfulness. 'That's very kind of you.' He fished in his pocket for a handful of change and paid the girl, then walked with her to the front door, giving Rosanna time to pull herself together.

Ewen stayed chatting to Sally Todd for a while, and by the time he came back his mood was vastly different.

'Sorry about the caveman tactics,' he said coolly. 'I'll drive you back now.'

'Thank you.'

He looked at his watch. 'I've delayed you, I'm afraid. I'd better drive you straight to Ealing.'

Rosanna shook her head. 'I can't go home looking like this. Just take me to the flat. I'll go by Underground to the Broadway.'

'Certainly not. It's my fault you're late. I'll drive you to the flat and wait for you.'

Ewen put the hood up on the car before they began what proved to be the most unbearable journey of Rosanna's entire life. Ewen talked, in the beginning with reason and intelligence, in the end with passionate force, on the subject of why they were meant to be lovers. That like Harry and Rose they belonged together. In vain Rosanna argued with him, pitting the years she'd had with David against the brief duration of her time with Ewen, which evoked such a stony silence from him, the rest of the journey was a nightmare. By the time they reached London Rosanna felt exhausted and miserable and desperate to get out of the car.

When they arrived at the flat Ewen found a parking space and remained with the car while Rosanna hurried inside to change her clothes for jeans and a plain white cotton shirt. She thrust her bare feet into navy deck shoes, and made a few lightning repairs to her face, tied her hair back with a white-dotted red scarf, snatched up her jacket and ran out to the car.

'Sorry to hold you up,' she panted as she slid into the car.

'Not at all. You were remarkably swift.' Ewen tossed his newspaper into the back of the car. 'Sally provided me with reading matter, remember.'

If his reminder of Sally's interruption was deliberate it was very successful. Rosanna's eyes kindled behind her dark glasses, but Ewen made no further reference to the episode as he drove, and said very little at all until Rosanna asked him to park a fair distance away from her home.

'Why?' he demanded. 'I'd like to meet your parents.'

'Well, you can't,' she said irritably. 'How can I explain away the fact that you're driving me there on a Sunday morning? *Please*, Ewen,' she entreated, but he ignored her and parked the car directly outside the house.

'Calm down,' he said, and walked with her up the drive. 'While we're alone, listen closely. I haven't changed my mind. As I've said before, I'm not Harry Manners, officer and gentleman. I refuse to let you ruin two lives.'

'Just one life—David's!' she retorted.

'You'll be wrecking three lives if you marry him.' Ewen's eyes clashed with hers. 'No man deserves a wife in love with someone else.'

'But I'm not—'

'You are!' he said, with such controlled violence, Rosanna recoiled.

'Ewen, please. Don't do this to me.'

'You mean you want a day's grace to work out more arguments to bring up tomorrow—that's if you're coming tomorrow, of course,' he added, eyeing her challengingly.

For a split second Rosanna was tempted to tell him she wasn't, tomorrow or any other day. It was exactly what she ought to do. But if she was going to Boston to see David she needed the rest of the money Ewen was paying her.

'I'll be there,' she said wearily.

His smile was triumphant. 'Good. I thought perhaps you might be afraid to work for me any more.'

'Why?'

'In case I go ape and try to force you into my bed again,' he said flippantly.

'I doubt that. After all, you didn't force me last night,' she said, and regretted it instantly at the look in Ewen's eyes.

He breathed in deeply. 'Do you think I need reminding? But don't worry, Rosanna. I take what's freely given, or nothing.'

'Please go,' she said desperately. 'My parents will be out here in a minute.'

'Don't look like that!' Ewen took her by the shoulders, bent his head and kissed her quivering mouth with a tenderness which cut her to pieces. 'All right, Rosanna, relax. I'm going. See you tomorrow.'

Ewen released her with undisguised reluctance, and Rosanna turned away blindly and began hunting in her bag for her key. Before she could find it the front door swung open, and Rosanna looked up with a bright smile intended for her mother, then froze, staring transfixed at the spectacularly handsome young giant who stood grinning at her sheepishly, his blond hair falling over his tanned forehead. For a split second all three of them were motion-less, like a tableau of ice sculptures, then Rosanna came to life.

'David!'

'Hi, Rosie.' He came bounding down the steps to give her a bear hug. 'Surprise, sur-prise. I went round to the flat, but no luck, so I came on here.'

At the look on Ewen's stony face Rosanna wished fervently that she could beam herself up to another planet. 'Why on *earth* didn't you let me know you were coming, David?' she demanded, then recollected herself hurriedly. 'This is Ewen Fraser, the author I've been working for. Ewen, this is David Norton.'

Rosanna, her head aching badly by this time, felt as if she were in the middle of a bad dream as the two men shook hands. They couldn't have been more different. Ewen was slimly built and lean, and although almost six feet tall he looked small in comparison to David Norton, who was half a head taller and built like an American football quarterback.

'I've heard a lot about you,' said Ewen smoothly, 'but I'm sure you both have a lot to catch up on so I'll take myself off.'

'Is that your Morgan?' said David eagerly, but Rosanna, knowing him of old, put a swift damper on any car-worship sessions.

'Goodbye, then, Ewen,' she said quickly. 'I'll see you in the morning. Thank you for driving me.'

'My pleasure.' Ewen nodded courteously at David. 'Very glad to have met you, Doctor. Goodbye, Rosanna.'

CHAPTER TEN

ROSANNA arrived very late in Chelsea next morning, and found Ewen's cleaner waiting to give her a letter from Ewen and a spare key.

Rosanna apologised for holding her up, but she knew that Ewen was out without being told. The house felt different. Empty. After Mrs Barker had taken herself off to her next job Rosanna stared for a long time at the letter, afraid to open it. When she did at last the contrast with his previous letters was painful.

Rosanna, it's best I work at the cottage from now on. I'll post the disks to you, and you can mail the draft pages back to me every day or two. Or you can finish right now, of course. It's up to you.

I apologise for taking advantage of the situation at the cottage, and for haranguing you so relentlessly on the journey home. Not having met with it before, I found rejection hard to take without a fight. Since then the situation has changed. Now I've met young Dr Norton in the spectacular flesh your reasons for preferring him to me are depressingly obvious. But take my advice, Rosanna; keep our lapse from grace to yourself.

If you intend going to the States immediately, let me know so that I can pay you what's owing. Ewen.

Rosanna sat down very carefully in her chair, staring blankly at the typewritten note. Had this actually been written by the man who'd made such passionate, heart-stopping love to her? It was a long time before she roused herself to make some coffee. When it was ready she gulped some down quickly, hoping the caffeine would stiffen her resolve, then dialled Ewen's number at the cottage.

At his curt bark of response she almost put the phone down.

'It's Rosanna,' she announced, brusque in her effort to keep her voice steady.

'Yes?'

'I've only just read your letter.'

'Then you arrived late this morning. Though in the circumstances,' he added abrasively, 'I suppose I should be grateful you came in at all.'

'I had a headache.'

'Hangover?'

'Certainly not.' She braced herself. 'Look, Ewen, I'd really like to carry on working until my part of the book is finished.'

'As you wish,' he said, after a lengthy pause.

'But I need to talk to you.'

'You are talking to me.'

'I meant in person.'

'I thought you'd be winging your way to America by this time. Is it urgent, or can you wait until the weekend?'

Her heart plummeted. 'Yes,' she said dully. 'I suppose so.'

'All right. I'll be at the house before you leave on Friday.'

'Thank you.'

'I was coming anyway. After you'd finished for the weekend, of course,' he added.

'Of course. Goodbye.' Rosanna put the phone down quickly, and poured herself another large, medicinal dose of caffeine.

The week that followed felt like the longest of Rosanna's life. No matter how hard she worked each day seemed endless, and the time dragged by so slowly she wondered if Friday would ever come. When it did Ewen arrived so late she was half demented by the time he put in an appearance, her worried greeting stifled at birth by the aloof, hostile look in his eyes.

'Hello, Rosanna,' he said coolly. 'Sorry to hold you up. The traffic was bad. I'm surprised you're still here.'

'Is that why you were late? Hoping I'd be gone?' she snapped, making no mention of her frantic worry for the past hour or so. Vivid images of the Morgan's mangled remains, and Ewen's inside it, had turned the endless wait into a nightmare.

Ewen threw down an overnight bag, then stood with arms folded. 'Well? What was so important that you had to see me in person to talk about it?'

Rosanna felt cold. Now they were face to face she was horribly afraid that her news wasn't important after all. 'I suppose I should have just told you over the phone,' she said quietly. 'I thought you might care to know that my—my arrangement with David is off.'

Ewen stood utterly still. 'Off?'

She nodded wordlessly, convinced now that her news wasn't the world-shaking pronouncement she'd thought it would be.

'You mean,' he said without expression, 'that you're not going to marry him?'

She nodded again, afraid to trust her voice.

Ewen looked at her in silence for so long that at last Rosanna could bear it no longer.

'I'd better go,' she muttered.

'Wait.'

Rosanna looked up to see a smile lifting one corner of Ewen's mouth.

'Come here,' he ordered.

But Rosanna couldn't move. Because her feet seemed nailed to the floor Ewen closed the space between them and seized her in his arms, kissing her with a ferocity she responded to by bursting into tears.

'Hey!' He held her away, smiling down into her streaming face. 'What's all this?'

'I thought for a minute you didn't care,' she sobbed, and buried her face against his chest.

He laughed unsteadily and held her close, one hand smoothing her hair. 'You know damn well I care, Rosanna. What the devil do I have to do to convince you?'

She lifted her head to look at him. 'For the past hour I've been going out of my mind,' she said hoarsely, 'imagining you dead in some accident in that beloved car of yours. Convince me you're alive, Ewen. Make love to me. Please?'

He let out a long, unsteady breath, then grabbed her by the hand, almost dragging her upstairs to his bedroom. 'I couldn't sleep for thinking of this,' he said roughly, and pinned her beneath him on the bed. He seized her hands and spread them wide. 'I escaped to the cottage because I couldn't trust myself to keep my hands off you if we were together here.'

'I thought you couldn't bear the sight of me any more,' she said, sniffing hard.

He rained kisses all over her wet face. 'All the way up tonight I kept wondering what the hell was so important that you had to tell me face to face.'

'Didn't you guess?' she said breathlessly.

'I didn't let myself. I just hoped, and called myself all kinds of fool for imagining it was even possible!' He kissed her with sudden, hot demand, and she trembled beneath him.

'I can't stop shaking,' she gasped.

'Neither can I.'

'I hope I'm not dreaming this, Ewen!'

'If you are I'm sharing the dream.' He smiled down into her glittering, tear-wet eyes. 'Let's make it come true.'

He began to make love to her with a passion fuelled by the misery of their separation. Her hair tossed back and forth on the pillow as she gloried in the sensations he was rousing in her body, their response to each other heightened to the point that when they reached the climax of their reconciliation the shared joy was so intense, the pleasure was almost pain.

Afterwards they stayed locked in each other's arms, Ewen's face buried in her tangled hair.

'Are you hungry?' he whispered, a long time later.

'Not really.' Rosanna tightened her arms as he drew away a little. 'I just want to lie here like this and pinch myself at intervals to make sure it's all true.'

He laughed, and kissed her nose, then moved his mouth down to hers, and slid his hand to cup the breast that rose, taut, to his touch. 'If we stay here, exactly like this, are you prepared for what will happen?'

For answer Rosanna slid the tip of her tongue delicately over his lips and wriggled closer, then they both jumped as the phone rang beside the bed.

Ewen swore under his breath, and barked his name into the receiver, then listened. 'Yes, she is. Hang on a second.' He gave the phone to Rosanna, pulling a face.

'Hello,' she said cautiously.

'Rosanna,' said Louise indignantly, 'have you forgotten we were going to see that new Tom Cruise film tonight?'

'Oh. Oh, dear. Yes, I had. Sorry, Lulu. I had some work to finish,' said Rosanna contritely, her face on fire at the gleam in Ewen's eyes.

'Nice work if you can get it, by the sound of it,' said her friend, cackling. 'All right, I'll toddle off with Paula, then. See you later? Or not?'

'I'll make the coffee when you come home,' promised Rosanna, and put the phone down, smiling at Ewen guiltily.

'A broken appointment?' he enquired, folding his arms behind his head. He grinned at her. 'The lady sounded indignant.'

'I was supposed to be back at the flat at seven. Then you came, and—' She smiled at him. 'I forgot all about Tom Cruise.'

'What greater compliment could a guy ask?' he said dryly, then slid out of bed and stretched unselfconsciously. 'I've got a plan for the rest of the evening. Want to hear it?'

Rosanna nodded happily. 'Yes, please.'

'I vote we send out for something to eat, then come back up here and make love until it's time for you to go home. If you must go home.'

'I must tonight,' she said with regret. 'But otherwise I love your plan. It's perfect.'

They ate tagliolini with meat sauce, accompanied by quantities of garlic bread, Rosanna wearing one of Ewen's shirts, and Ewen in a towelling robe as they sat cross-legged on the bed.

'You look a lot better in that than I do,' he told her, grinning as he watched her mop up the sauce with her bread. 'Very ladylike!'

'I was hungry,' she said with dignity. 'I haven't been eating well lately.'

'Why?'

'You know why!'

Ewen smiled, and leaned across to lick some sauce from the corner of her mouth, and Rosanna turned her head so that his tongue slid between her lips as they kissed.

'It's a good thing we both like garlic bread,' he said hoarsely as he drew away.

'True.' She frowned seriously. 'I don't think I could fancy a man who didn't like garlic.'

'You fancy me, then?'

'You bet your life I do,' she said, and took his plate from him to put it on the floor with hers. She smiled at him slowly. 'Want me to show you?'

It was late by the time they'd shared a bath together, and Rosanna was dressed again and respectable enough for the drive back in the taxi.

'I'd rather drive you myself,' said Ewen as they went downstairs to wait for it.

'In which case you should have eschewed the champagne.' Rosanna giggled, feeling drunk with love. 'Good word, eschewed.'

'On the other hand I can cuddle you all the way to your flat in the back seat, my lovely one.' He sighed. 'And then I'll come back to my lonely bed on my own.'

She smiled at him with her heart in her eyes, and he lifted her from the last step up into his arms and held her close, her feet swinging clear of the floor. 'Have you any idea how I feel right now, Rosanna Carey?'

'If it's anything like the way I feel,' she said breathlessly, 'just wonderful!'

He bit gently on her earlobe. 'You know, I took one look at that good-looking hunk of a doctor of yours that night and tried to accept defeat. I never thought in a million years you'd give him his marching orders and settle for me instead.'

Rosanna's eyes dropped, and Ewen set her on her feet, frowning.

'What? Speak, woman!'

'I don't really want to tell you this,' she muttered. 'In fact I should have said it the moment I saw you, but—'

'But I was in too much of a hurry to take you to bed,' he said, eyes narrowed. 'I take the blame. But don't keep me in suspense, darling. What should you have told me?'

Rosanna squared her shoulders and looked him in the eye. 'I didn't give David his marching orders,' she blurted. 'It was the other way about. David flew home to tell me he's met someone else. Like you said, doctors often marry doctors. The lady works at the same Boston hospital, and they're getting married next month. He came home to see his parents and talk to me at the same time. He felt he couldn't tell me in a letter or over the phone. He wanted to break the news in person.'

Ewen stood very still, the animation draining from his face. 'How very noble of him,' he said, in a tone which turned Rosanna's blood cold. 'And how fortunate you had me in reserve. Not first choice, of course, but I mustn't complain. One can't have everything.'

'Ewen, please, I haven't finished. Let me explain—'

'You already have. And I wish to God you hadn't,' he said savagely. 'Did you mention that you had me as second string?'

'No—but it wasn't like that!'

'It was exactly like that. It's flatteringly obvious, after the evening we've just spent, that you ''fancy'' me. But that's not enough for me, Rosanna. And while you still had David in view it wasn't enough for you, either. You weren't prepared to throw him over in exchange for me.' Ewen flung away in sudden rage. 'I could see why the minute I laid eyes on him. He's taller than me, bigger than me, and looks like a bloody film star.' He turned on her in sudden menace. 'Is he a better lover than me, too?'

Rosanna backed away. 'It was never like that with David.'

'Why? Don't tell me Mr Perfect falls short in the sex department!'

'No, he doesn't,' she said hotly. 'Ewen, please. Try to understand. I met David when we were both very young. We were just friends in the beginning. The other part just sort of—evolved.'

Ewen eyed her in distaste. 'Oh, I understand, Rosanna. It's insultingly obvious that whatever you had with Norton was too good to pass up for what you had with me!'

'You *don't* understand,' she said in despair. 'If you'd just let me finish—'

'You don't have to. I already know the story,' said Ewen scornfully. 'You couldn't jilt your doctor in case it ruined his life. You don't honestly believe that a man with his attractions would have gone unconsoled for long?' His eyes blazed into hers. 'Or were you obsessed with some crazy idea about emulating Rose Norman's sacrifice?'

'Of course I wasn't!' Suddenly Rosanna lost her temper. 'Shut up and listen, Ewen Fraser. In the beginning I resented you because you were thinking of Rose when you looked at me. And I was jealous, heaven help me, because you were in love with a ghost—'

'Utter nonsense!' he interrupted harshly, but she held up her hand.

'Hear me out. That day in the lift changed everything. I had no idea I could behave like that, feel like that. It was a revelation. And when you made love to me at last, at the cottage, it surpassed anything I'd ever imagined. But it made me frightened. I was sure it couldn't last. Too hot not to cool down, and all that. Because there was no question of marriage I was afraid to throw away my future with David for a love affair that would burn itself out one day.'

Ewen raked a hand through his hair, glaring at her. 'The boot was on the other foot, though, wasn't it? It was this unswerving devotion of Norton's that died a death.'

Her chin lifted. 'It's not like that. David still loves me in his own way—'

'Does he really? To hell with the doctor's feelings. It's my own that concern me right at this moment, and they feel as though they've been trampled on.' His eyes bored into hers with such hostility, she shrank away involuntarily. 'I like to win, Rosanna Carey. To come first. I can't handle the role of runner-up.'

'Will you let me *finish*—?'

'No! You've said enough.' Ewen looked up in obvious relief as the doorbell rang, and brushed past her, his body taut with anger as he made for the door to speak to the taxi driver.

By this time Rosanna was so furious, she wanted to hit him. 'All right, I'm going. I'm up-to-date with the disks I've had so far, in case you're worried.'

'I finished the first draft today,' he said shortly.

'Really?' she said, diverted for an instant.

'One way and another,' he said with sarcasm, 'I forgot to mention it.'

'You must be pleased.'

'I'll deliver a verdict when the book is finished.'

'Ewen—' she began, but he shook his head.

'Just go, Rosanna.'

'*Right*,' she said in sudden fury. 'I will. And I'm not coming back.'

'Fine,' he snapped, his eyes narrowed to furious gold slivers.

Rosanna looked at him blankly, hiding her horrified disbelief. Telling him she was leaving for good had been a last, desperate throwing down of the gauntlet. But it had failed. Ewen Fraser was actually going to let her walk out of his life.

'Goodbye, then,' she said with hauteur.

'Goodbye.'

Ewen slammed the door shut the moment she was outside, and Rosanna got into the waiting taxi, feeling as though the bottom had dropped out of her world.

After a night of unrelieved misery it was dawn before Rosanna slept, and she woke late next morning to find Louise sitting on her bed, offering a mug of tea.

'Thanks,' croaked Rosanna. 'What time is it?'

'Tennish.' Louise handed over the mug, then got to her feet, an odd expression on her face as she hovered.

'What's up?' asked Rosanna without interest. The events of the night before were already flooding her with such renewed misery she had no attention to spare for Louise's incessant man-problems. I'm the one with problems this time, she thought bitterly. 'Shouldn't you be getting ready for lunch with Lawrence?'

'It's early yet.'

'Right. I'll be up in a minute. How long has David got before taking off for Heathrow?'

Louise hugged her arms across her chest. 'Not long, thank goodness. Personally, Ro, I'm amazed you let him stay last night.'

'Why? He came out of his way to say goodbye on his way to the States. It saved him a hotel room.' She drank some tea.

'I don't know how you could bear to know he's dumped you for someone else!' Louise chewed on a finger. 'The thing is, Rosanna, he answered the door just now.'

'So?'

'Ewen Fraser called to bring your raincoat back. You left it behind yesterday.'

Rosanna stared in utter horror. 'And David opened the door to him?'

Louise nodded glumly. 'Wearing only a smile and a towel—he'd just got out of the bath. Someone left by the main door as Ewen arrived, so he came straight down to ours.'

Rosanna shuddered. 'Break it to me gently—what happened?'

'Nothing much. Your author explained very briefly, handed over the raincoat and left. In a hurry, David said— Rosanna! Don't look like that. Oh, dear, come here—let me give you a hug.'

Later, when Rosanna had showered, dressed, and regained something of the will to live, she went into the sitting room to find Louise had taken sanctuary in her room, well away from the line of fire. David was waiting for her, ready to go.

'I'm off, then, Rosie. By the way, this guy Fraser you've been working for called to bring your raincoat back.' David eyed her warily. 'Does he come here much?'

'No,' said Rosanna shortly. 'Today was the first time.'

'Are you in love with him?' he asked, eyeing her pallor.

'Why should you think that?'

David smiled his toothpaste-ad smile. 'Louise dropped the odd hint or three. She went for me like a wildcat because I greeted the famous author in my skin, so to speak. Fraser wasn't exactly overjoyed, either—went off in a bit of a strop.'

'You're exaggerating,' she said curtly.

'No way.' David wagged a finger at her. 'It explains a lot. No wonder you took my news so calmly, Rosie.'

'How did you expect me to take it?' she said scornfully. 'Tearing my hair, and begging you not to abandon me? I was just being civilised, David.'

'If you say so. Anyway, thanks for letting me stay last night.' He reached for her but Rosanna backed away.

'Time you were going, David,' she said briskly.

He looked down at her, regret mingled with affection in the bright blue eyes. 'I just wanted to say my feelings for you aren't changed, Rosie.'

'I realise that.' She smiled wryly. 'Mine aren't changed for you, either. I was just a tad mistaken about them both, unfortunately. You and I had a loving friendship, David. But in the end it wasn't enough. For either of us.'

He shook his head. 'It was all I ever wanted. Until I met Holly.' He hesitated, then took out his wallet. 'I've got a picture. Do you want to see it?'

'Of course,' said Rosanna, thawing, expecting to see a gorgeous, long-legged blonde. But the girl in the photograph was wearing the white coat of her calling, with no legs visible, her brown hair pinned severely back, and she looked tired. But her smile was warm in her clear-cut, clever face, and to Rosanna's surprise she found she liked the look of Holly very much. 'She's lovely.'

'She's tall, too,' said David with a grin. 'I don't have to bend double to kiss her.'

Rosanna managed a laugh, and David took her hand, looking remorseful. 'I didn't get a chance to explain to your man. Sorry.'

'He's not my man.'

'Pull the other one!' David bent down to kiss her cheek, then winked over her shoulder as Louise made a very wary entrance into the room. 'It's OK, Lulu. No bloodshed. I'm on my way.'

When he'd gone Rosanna slumped down on the sofa, wondering whether to ring Ewen. 'He took one look at David and jumped to the wrong conclusion, of course. Should I try to explain?'

'I could kick myself,' said Louise angrily. 'If only I'd answered the door—'

'It's not your fault.'

'I'm so *sorry*, Rosanna. You really like this man Fraser, don't you?'

'No, I don't *like* him, I'm mad about him.' She managed a shaky smile. 'Not that it matters. If Ewen's convinced I let David share my bed last night for auld lang syne I'm hardly likely to be seeing him again.'

CHAPTER ELEVEN

IN THE end Rosanna decided to take the bull by the horns and ring the Chelsea house, but the only reward for her courage was Ewen's recorded message. She asked him to ring her back, then tried the cottage, but he wasn't there either. Or if he was he wasn't answering the phone. She left the same message, and spent most of the weekend waiting for a call that never came. In the end Rosanna's misery gave way to a deep, abiding anger. Ewen, she thought fiercely, wasn't the only one with pride.

Her mother, who now knew most of the story, advised a change of scene. 'You've got plenty of time before you start at the school,' she pointed out. 'Use the money for a holiday, as you originally meant to.'

'Where do you suggest I go?' Rosanna's smile was wry. 'Boston's no longer an option.'

'How about a trip to see Sam in Sydney?' Mrs Carey smiled coaxingly. 'He's got a nice spare room in his house in Bondi. He'll only be free at weekends, of course, but you can go sightseeing in the week on your own. Maybe take a trip up to the Barrier Reef, like we did.'

Rosanna eyed her mother in surprise for a moment, then said slowly, 'I think that's probably a quite brilliant idea. I'll ring Sam in the morning.'

During the course of the weekend Rosanna came to terms with the fact that she'd been right about Ewen all along. The flare of passion between them had been too sudden and too fierce to last. This trip would serve as therapy. A cure for the longing that still burned inside her at the thought of his hands and mouth, of his lean, taut body compelling hers towards such dizzying peaks of ecstasy, she still trembled in the night at the memory of it.

During the long hours of the flight to Sydney, Rosanna had plenty of time for reflection. She knew, now, that it would have been a disaster to marry David. But it was rather funny that her original idea of sticking to her quixotic guns had been an unwanted sacrifice after all. Sacrifice? She frowned suddenly as she stared at the brilliant sky through the window. Was Ewen right, after all? Surely she hadn't been trying to live up to Rose!

A suntanned, thinner Rosanna returned from her holiday on a late August Sunday morning to a warm reception from her parents at Heathrow.

'Sam's fine, I loved Sydney, but it's great to be home.' She hugged her mother and father in turn, and on the way from the airport talked nonstop. 'I dragged Sam to Sydney Opera House, visited the prisons they've made into museums, and went to that fabulous fish restaurant you told me about.'

'I'm glad you enjoyed it, darling,' said her mother, looking relieved.

'I did. It was just what I needed.' Rosanna was enthusiastic as she described her trip to Port Douglas with Sam to marvel at the wonders of the Great Barrier Reef, including a trip in a glass-sided boat to marvel at coral banks and exotic, translucent fish and stingrays, huge marine turtles, even the occasional shark. 'It was an amazing experience.'

'We thought you'd enjoy it. You look a lot better than the girl we put on the plane to Sydney,' observed her father. 'By the way, Ewen Fraser came round last week. He brought your mother flowers, and thanked her for letting him see Rose's papers, and all that. He's finished the book.'

'Oh, good,' said Rosanna, determinedly casual to cover her reaction to the mere mention of Ewen's name.

'He was a bit behind schedule, apparently,' said Mrs Carey.

'Because I left him to finish it on his own?'

'No, but I'll give you the details when we get home,' said her mother, and gave Rosanna a look which meant she would prefer the conversation left until they were alone, since John Carey was blissfully ignorant of his daughter's feelings for Ewen Fraser.

By the time her father had gone upstairs after lunch for a nap, Rosanna could contain her curiosity no longer.

'Why was Ewen behind with the book?' she asked.

'He had an accident—''

'In the Morgan?' said Rosanna in horror.

'No, on the way to the Underground,' said her mother in swift reassurance. 'When Ewen was leaving your place the day he brought your raincoat back, one of those motorcycle couriers ran into him and knocked him over. Don't look like that, darling. Ewen's fine. Now. His only injury was a broken ankle, and concussion. He hit his head on the pavement. He was kept in hospital for a couple of days, then his parents collected him and took him home with them to convalesce.'

'So that's why he didn't ring back,' said Rosanna, feeling limp. 'Is he back in his own place now?'

'I think so.' Henrietta Carey smiled, and patted her daughter's hand. 'He said he rang you at the flat, but Louise told him you'd gone to Australia. He came round to invite us to lunch last weekend with his parents and his grandmother.'

Rosanna's eyes widened in surprise. 'Did you go?'

'Of course we did! I was dying to meet Alice. What a character! We got on like a house on fire. With Mary and Alec Fraser, too,' added Mrs Carey. 'You made quite an impression on them. They were annoyed with Ewen because he hadn't taken you back to see them again.'

Rosanna felt quite unable to cope with all this. The shock of Ewen's accident rendered her jet-lagged brain incapable of anything other than relief that he hadn't been seriously hurt.

'He asked me to explain why he hadn't returned your calls,' said her mother, and took Rosanna in her arms. 'Go on. Cry.'

With only a short time to go before she started teaching again Rosanna decided to move back into the flat after a couple of days in Ealing. But there would be no more phone calls to Ewen Fraser. The ball was now firmly in his court. She had every excuse to ring him, it was true, if only to ask about his health. But she wasn't going to. If he wanted to see her he could ring and say so. And if he didn't it wasn't the end of the world. She would survive. Just as her grandmother had done before her.

Later that evening Rosanna was ironing in front of the television when the buzzer rang on the intercom. She spoke into it and leaned against the wall, her knees trembling when she heard Ewen's voice.

'I rang your parents to ask if you were back, Rosanna. They said you were here. I need to talk to you.'

'Come down, then.' She pressed the release button, wishing vainly that she were wearing something more presentable than the brief, striped singlet dress she'd bought on holiday.

Ewen greeted her very formally when she opened the door. He looked drawn and tired. His hair was untidy as usual, but he was wearing a dark city suit, and at the sight of him Rosanna wanted to throw her arms round him and hug him to death. Instead she greeted him politely and asked him to come in.

'Do sit down. You won't mind if I go on ironing?'

Ewen looked slightly taken aback. 'No, not at all.' He limped slightly, she noticed, as he crossed the room to sit on the sofa.

'How are you?' she asked, her eyes on the silk shirt she was ironing. 'My parents told me about your accident. Are you fully recovered now?'

'In time I'll be good as new for the most part.' He leaned back in the chair, his eyes riveted to the length of bare brown leg on view. 'I'm sorry I didn't return your calls, Rosanna. When I came out of hospital I rang the house to access my messages. But by then you were on your way to Australia.'

She gave him a friendly, impersonal smile. 'Not to worry.'

Ewen looked at her levelly. 'Was it something important?'

'It seemed so at the time.' She hung the blouse up and took another from the basket.

'But not any more,' he said grimly.

Rosanna shrugged. 'It's quite a while since then. Things have a way of working themselves out, given time.' She looked up, then frowned as she realised Ewen looked alarm-ingly pale. 'What's the matter?'

'Headache,' he admitted. 'Not a hangover this time. Since my head met the pavement that day I get them fairly often. I'm assured it's only temporary.'

'I do hope so,' she said politely. 'It must be hell to stare at a computer screen with a blind-ing headache.'

'Did your mother tell you I'd finished the first draft?' he asked.

'Yes. Are you pleased with it?'

'Not yet. I've altered it quite a bit. I should have the second version ready any day now.' He winced suddenly.

'Would you like some painkillers?' she asked gently.

'I would, indeed. Thanks.'

'Look in the cabinet over the washbasin in the bathroom, first on your left down the hall. Several types there; take your pick. I'll make some tea.'

Rosanna folded away the ironing board and put it in the cupboard in the hall, wondering if Ewen was all right. In the kitchen, a rather grand description for the cooker and fridge hidden behind a screen, she made a pot of tea, and found a packet of plain biscuits, experiencing a strong feeling of *déjà vu*. Only this time Ewen's pain was due to something far worse than a hangover.

It was some time before he rejoined her, looking even more haggard than before. 'Sorry to take so long.'

'Do sit down. Did you take some pills?'

Ewen nodded, then grimaced, regretting it.

'Can you manage a biscuit?' she said coaxingly, offering the plate.

He ate one with care, then drank gratefully from the cup she handed him, but clenched his jaw as the heat of the tea made the pounding in his head worse for a moment. Rosanna watched him anxiously over the rim of her cup.

'Shouldn't you see a doctor?' she asked after a while.

'No. I've had my fill of doctors lately. One way and another,' he added with sudden, bitter emphasis. 'But that's enough about me. I want to know about *you*, Rosanna.'

'I'm fine. I had a great time in Australia with Sam. And without him. I did a lot of sightseeing.'

'Good. I'm glad you enjoyed it. But I haven't come to talk about your holiday.' His eyes met hers with an impaling look. 'I'm asking about your health. You've lost weight.'

She shrugged. 'It was quite a hectic holiday, but I'm very well. I think I look rather good with a suntan.' She smiled a little. 'Though I wouldn't be displaying quite so much of it if I'd expected company.'

Ewen downed the rest of his tea as if it were a dose of medicine. 'Why did you want me to ring back so urgently, Rosanna?'

She curled up on a chair. 'So I could do some explaining. About the last time you were here for one thing, though there was something else. At the time it seemed real life-or-death stuff to explain.'

His mouth twisted. 'You mean my encounter with your naked ex-lover.'

'I thought he was wearing a towel.'

'It fell off when he took the raincoat I shoved at him.'

'Oh.'

There was silence for a moment.

'Not that it matters now, but it wasn't quite the way it looked,' she said at last. 'David came to say goodbye on his way to Heathrow. And, before you ask, he'd just come out of the bath after spending the night on our floor.'

'Why the floor?' asked Ewen politely.

Rosanna waved a hand at the small sofa. 'He doesn't fit on that.'

'I meant,' he said deliberately, 'why not in your bed?'

'I know you did,' she said evenly. 'He spent the night on the floor because it seemed pointless to send him to a hotel when he could stay here. David and I are still friends, Ewen, whoever he, or I, should happen to marry. I'm afraid I wasn't very good company for his last night in London. Not after the way you sent me packing. I pleaded a headache in the end and went to bed. Alone.' Her eyes locked with his. 'I'm amazed you could think otherwise after the evening we'd just spent together, Ewen.'

His mouth twisted. 'I realised that, once I came round, days later. But after confrontation with a naked Hercules that morning I stormed off to the Underground in such blind fury I never saw the lad on the bike. I woke up in Casualty a fair time later, and the rest you know. The courier escaped with only a bruise or two, thank God.'

'So I'm to blame?' she asked.

'Of course not! I was so obsessed with wanting to knock Norton's perfect teeth down his throat I didn't look where I was going. Simple as that.'

Rosanna pulled a face. 'David said you were— put out.'

'Put out? I was off my head with jealousy.' He smiled his familiar, lop-sided smile. 'We're back to the testosterone again. The two main outlets available to the male of the species are fighting or making love. That day I was out of luck on both counts.'

'I sympathise on one of them,' said Rosanna dryly. 'When Louise told me what happened I could have murdered David myself.'

'Is that true?' he said, brightening.

'Yes. Which I would have told you, if I could have found you.'

'Was that the only reason for wanting to talk to me?' said Ewen, sitting up straighter. His eyes met hers compellingly. 'Are you being honest with me, Rosanna?'

She frowned, pushing her hair back behind her ears. 'Of course I am. I was desperate to put you straight about David. But when you didn't get in touch I gave up in the end. Thought you weren't interested. So, thanks to you, I took myself off to Australia.'

'As far away from me as you could get,' he said bitterly.

'I meant the salary you paid me made the trip possible, Ewen. I went to visit my brother, Sam.'

'I know.' He frowned. 'Which reminds me. I owe you some money. I didn't pay you up to date.'

Rosanna stiffened. 'Is that why you came here tonight?'

'Of course it isn't,' he said irritably. 'I've only just thought of it. One way and another I haven't been firing on all cylinders lately.'

'When Mother said you'd had an accident I thought you were in the Morgan,' she said, not looking at him.

'Damn good thing I wasn't. If I'd been driving things could have been a lot worse.'

'The thought had occurred to me.'

Ewen was silent for a moment, then he got to his feet, looking down at her with such urgency in his eyes, Rosanna jumped up in alarm.

'What is it? Do you feel ill?'

'No. I just want you to tell me the truth, Rosanna.'

She frowned, puzzled. 'But I have. David stayed the night, that's all—'

'I don't give a damn about David,' grated Ewen, and seized her hands. 'Are you pregnant, Rosanna?'

Rosanna stared at him, aghast, then wrenched her hands away. 'Certainly not.'

'You mean you're going to keep it secret from me?'

'I don't know what you're talking about.'

'Oh, yes, you do!' He grasped her by the shoulders, his fingers digging into her skin.

'I've just been in your bathroom. There's a pregnancy testing kit in your cabinet, next to the aspirin.'

'You're hurting me,' she said coldly, and he dropped his hands.

'So either you're pregnant and you already know, or you haven't made the test yet because you're afraid you are,' he said with certainty. 'Was this why you were so desperate to contact me?'

Rosanna eyed him with distaste. 'Your knock on the head has addled your brains, Ewen Fraser. Those phone calls were made only a week or so after—after—'

'We first made love together,' he finished for her.

'Exactly. It was a bit soon for any doubts on that particular score. Besides which,' she added with sudden heat, 'you were very careful to protect me—and yourself—from any possible consequences. So if you think I'm pregnant you must assume someone else is responsible.'

'No!' He raked a hand through his hair, and winced as his head protested. 'I was half asleep in the night when I began to make love to you again at the cottage. By the time I was fully awake I was too much overtaken with—'

'Lust?' she said sweetly.

'Longing, desire, or anything else in the thesaurus you fancy,' he bit back. 'Whatever it was I realised afterwards I'd been careless. So tell me the truth. Are you expecting my child?'

'No, I am not!' Rosanna's stomach muscles clenched at the thought. 'Don't worry. There's no embarrassing little sequel to our short-lived encounter. Which is just as well. Picture your reaction,' she went on with sarcasm, 'if I'd confided that kind of secret to you the moment you came through the door tonight. Would you have really believed the baby was yours—and not David's?'

Ewen looked as though she'd punched him in the stomach. 'If you'd said it was, yes,' he said slowly. 'Of course I'd have believed you.'

'You don't sound totally convinced.'

'I am.' Ewen looked down at her broodingly. 'I wish you *were* pregnant.'

'Do you indeed? I don't,' she snapped.

'It would make things simpler at this point.'

'How?'

His eyes glittered suddenly. 'If you were I'd drag you home with me before you had time to draw breath.'

She glared at him, incensed. 'I'd like to see you try!'

Ewen's arms went out, then dropped as she backed away. 'Rosanna. Don't. I want you so much I—'

'Yes. I know. You told me that before.' She ignored the trembling in her midriff at the urgency in his voice. 'But you still can't really handle the fact that David came first. Admit it.'

'You're a teacher. You could help me learn very quickly,' he said, advancing on her with an unsettling air of purpose.

'But I'm not going to,' she retorted, scrambling back out of reach.

'Why do you refuse to admit we're made for each other?' he said, and caught her as she dodged behind the sofa, holding her by the wrists. 'You can't get away from me in here, my girl, so listen. I was going to do everything by the book tonight. I even dressed up in a suit for the occasion, prepared to go down on one knee, determined to bring you round to my way of thinking and persuade you to move in with me—tonight, preferably.'

Rosanna had been ready to throw herself in his arms and say yes at one point, but his closing sentence stifled her assent before she made it. Marriage, as usual, was not Ewen's intention. Savage disappointment made her want to lash out at him with her fists, but she had better weapons in her armoury than that.

'But, Ewen,' she said very distinctly, 'last time we met you couldn't cope with being my second choice. Wouldn't even hear me out when I tried to explain—'

'I've changed my mind,' he said harshly, his eyes glittering down into hers. 'I don't care any more. I want you, Rosanna. And, unless you're the greatest actress outside of Hollywood, you feel the same about me. I just won't let you condemn us both to the separation Rose imposed on Harry.'

She glared up into the slanted eyes with open hostility. 'And that, really, is what it's all about, isn't it? A sort of reincarnation of Harry and Rose's doomed love affair. Would you be so hot to get me in your bed if I didn't look like her? Of course not,' she said scornfully. 'It's been down to Rose right from the first. You want to re-enact her romance with Harry. Well, I'm not Rose. I'm me, Rosanna, and I'm turning your offer down, Ewen Fraser. I refuse to share my life with a ghost.'

Ewen released her hands, his face inscrutable. 'Is that final?'

'Yes,' she said flatly.

He took dark-lensed aviator glasses from his pocket and put them on. 'If it wasn't for this pain in my head I might stay and try to argue you out of it. But throwing up on your carpet is hardly likely to further my cause. May I ring for a taxi?'

'You don't need to. They cruise down this road all the time.'

'I won't trouble you any longer, then.'

Rosanna walked to the door and opened it. 'Goodbye, Ewen.'

He paused, his expression hidden behind the dark lenses. 'Just one thing, Rosanna. Why *is* there a pregnancy test kit in your bathroom?'

'It's absolutely no business of yours,' she said coldly, 'but it belongs to someone who rented my room here for a while. She wasn't obliged to use it, as it happens. But thank you for reminding me. I'll get rid of it before the next man in my life gets any wrong ideas.'

'All right, put your knife away,' said Ewen malevolently, and brushed past her. At the foot of the stairs he turned before she could go inside. 'Good luck with the new job.'

'Thank you,' said Rosanna, and slammed the door in his face. She waited, tense, for a moment, but there was no knock, and at last she threw herself down on the sofa, fists clenched, determined not to cry. She was shedding no more tears over Ewen Fraser. Or any other man.

It took Rosanna no time at all to discover that pride was a very poor bedfellow. The glow from her holiday disappeared so quickly she was obliged to tell her mother a little of what had happened to allay Henrietta Carey's worry.

'It's quite simple, really,' she said without emotion. 'I look so much like Rose he can't quite detach me from the girl his uncle loved. I'm sure he just wants to re-enact their love affair all over again. With me.'

'That sounds very unlikely, darling,' said her mother, frowning. 'Is that why he came to see you?'

Rosanna nodded. 'At first he couldn't cope because I couldn't bring myself to break with David—'

'Which is understandable!'

'Yes. I know. But then he cast his scruples aside, ready to forget that.'

'Why?'

Rosanna looked away. 'Because he wants me to live with him and be his love, and all that.'

Mrs Carey looked thoughtful. 'And you didn't fancy that?'

Rosanna smiled humourlessly. 'Actually I did. A lot. But on a different kind of basis. I'm a conventional girl at heart, Mother. Funny, old-fashioned creature that I am. Marriage or nothing, that's me. Ewen's idea was a bit less permanent.'

'Are you in love with him?'

'Oh, yes,' said Rosanna drearily. 'I thought my trip to Australia might have cured me of that. But two seconds in Mr Fraser's company the other night put me right on that score.'

'You're mad,' said Mrs Carey with conviction. 'If you want him, why on earth give him his marching orders?'

'That, Mother, darling, is a question I've been asking myself ever since.'

'Swallow your pride and ring him.'

Rosanna took her mother's advice and rang the Chelsea number first thing next morning. The phone was picked up after the second ring, but it was Mrs Barker who answered.

'Hello, Mrs B. This is Rosanna.'

'Hello, dear, how are you? Mr Fraser's not here. He's in the country again. You can ring him at the cottage.'

She would do better than that, thought Rosanna. She would borrow her mother's car for the drive to Long Ashley, and beard the literary lion in his den. She needed to talk to Ewen face to face.

She left next morning, a little after rush hour. The weather was fine and the traffic no heavier than usual, but Rosanna was no fan of motorway travel. She was glad to turn off eventually into the maze of minor roads she'd marked in red on the map. The journey seemed endless, but just as she felt certain she was lost she found the narrow, tree-lined road she remembered so well. But when the familiar stone wall came into view Rosanna drove past Ewen's cottage, unable to bring herself to turn into his driveway and park, uninvited. She found a lay-by a little further on and left the car in the shade of an overhanging tree.

The walk back was longer than it looked, and Rosanna felt very hot and untidy by the time she reached the cottage. For a moment she was tempted to turn tail and drive straight back to London, but now she was so near at last the need to see Ewen overcame any misgivings. She opened the gate and walked slowly up the path, her shoes crunching on the gravel. After she knocked on the door there was no sound for a while, then at last, just as she was about to leave, she heard footsteps on the stairs. But when the door opened, to Rosanna's horror it was Sally Todd who peered round it, hair in wild disarray, one of Ewen's robes clutched round her naked body.

'Oh, it's you,' she said rudely, holding the door wider. 'Are you expected?'

'No,' said Rosanna with effort. 'Hello, Sally. Is Mr Fraser in?'

The girl eyed her with open hostility. 'I'll just pop back to his bedroom and tell him you're here, shall I?'

Rosanna felt so sick she almost turned tail and ran while the girl went back upstairs. But pride exerted iron control over her rebelling stomach and she stood her ground, determined not to give Ewen the satisfaction of running away like a coward. She heard Sally talking, and a muffled male voice answering, then the girl reappeared, strutting down the stairs in crude imitation of a model on a catwalk.

Sally smiled triumphantly, and stretched her hands up to hold her hair away from her neck, displaying a small purple bruise of unmistakable provenance. She winked lewdly. 'He says he's too busy to see you, miss.'

CHAPTER TWELVE

THE Beaumont School for Girls was less than two miles away from Rosanna's flat, and from the first she made it a habit to run to school every morning, and back again in the evening, regardless of the weather. She threw herself into the task of teaching English to the girls in the junior school, and agreed readily when asked to help put on the school play, supervise school outings, or perform any other extra task that came her way. She ran hard and worked hard, socialised as much as possible, tired herself out in the process. But never enough to erase the memory of the degrading episode at Ewen Fraser's cottage.

To keep the memory mint-fresh, the paperback version of *Savage Dawn* came out not long after Rosanna started work at the school, and every bookshop she passed displayed Ewen's best-selling novel, sometimes with accompanying blown-up portraits of the author.

But fate had worse tricks up her sleeve. One memorable weekend Rosanna was browsing in a West End department store with Louise when she spotted Ewen Fraser seated at a table signing books for the people lining up to buy them. She stopped dead, bumping into Louise, who protested loudly enough for Ewen to look up and see them. He shot to his feet, but Rosanna turned blindly and made for the entrance at such speed, Louise was panting when she caught up with her outside.

'Steady on, Ro! I'm not as fit as you. Gosh, your author's even tastier than he looks in his photographs. No wonder you're pining. Are you sure you want to run away?'

'Dead certain,' said Rosanna tersely, and hurried Louise away just in case Ewen came in pursuit. This wasn't fair, she thought wildly, in misery which deepened when it became obvious that Ewen had no intention of coming after her.

'I wish you'd tell me what *happened* at his cottage,' panted Louise crossly.

'No way.'

'Did he try and rape you or something?'

'Certainly not. Let's change the subject. *Please!*'

Louise shrugged philosophically, squeezed Rosanna's hand, and nobly made no protest when her friend wanted to go straight home.

Rosanna was in the bath later when Louise came in to announce there was a phone call from someone at the school.

'Did you say I'd ring back?'

'I didn't dare. They're holding on.'

Rosanna wrapped herself in a towel and went along the hall to pick up the phone.

'Rosanna, don't hang up,' said Ewen peremptorily.

She made a choked sound of disgust and slammed the receiver down, then fled back to the bathroom, colliding with Louise in the hall.

'You knew who it was!' she accused, eyes flashing.

'Yes, I did.' Louise pulled a face. 'But Ro, you're so miserable underneath. After seeing Ewen Fraser in the flesh today I couldn't hang up on the man.'

'Next time—if there *is* a next time—tell him I never, ever want to talk to him again. Understood?'

'All right, all right, keep your hair on.'

Next day, when John Carey was dozing in front of a football match on television after lunch, his wife beckoned Rosanna into the kitchen.

'Ewen rang last night, darling.'

'What did he want?' said Rosanna stonily.

'He *said* he wanted to bring back Rose's belongings. But what he really wanted was to ask about you.' Mrs Carey gave a troubled sigh. 'Obviously something so bad happened at his cottage that day you can't even talk about it. And I feel responsible, because I urged you to get in touch with him. I interfered, and I'm sorry.'

Rosanna put her arms round her mother, leaning her head on the familiar, loved shoulder. 'It wasn't your fault.'

'Ewen saw you yesterday, I gather.'

'He was signing books. I was shopping with Louise.'

'And,' went on Mrs Carey, 'he rang you last night.'

'I wouldn't speak to him.'

'So he said. Darling, I know what I just said about interfering, but just this once, couldn't you at least talk to Ewen?'

Rosanna detached herself, and looked her mother in the eye. 'No. Not this once. Not ever.'

Before long Rosanna was beginning to feel part of the school, and had made new friends on the staff. Little by little life grew more bearable, partly because after two more unsuccessful attempts to speak to her there had been no more calls from Ewen.

'And thank heaven for that,' said Louise with feeling. 'I hate playing pig-in-the-middle. But I think you're mad not to let him talk to you once, at least.'

Rosanna was in the staffroom drinking coffee with some of her colleagues at break one morning when Jane Rowlands, the history teacher, came in, eyes sparkling with excitement, to announce that the entire staff was required in the hall the following Friday evening for an extra lecture.

There was a concerted groan.

'The good news,' went on Jane, undeterred, 'is the identity of the speaker.'

'Not something to do with computers again!' said someone bitterly.

'No. *Much* better. It's Ewen Fraser, the author of that novel on the Zulu Wars. He was on one of those television talk shows last week. *Very* nice. The Upper Sixth will froth at the mouth when they clap eyes on him!'

Rosanna ran back to the flat in half her usual time later that afternoon, wishing she could break a leg, even get mugged in the park. All the way home she dreamed up excuses about stomach upsets, migraines, flu, vital appointments elsewhere—anything to avoid attending Ewen Fraser's lecture. But by the time she reached home she was resigned to the inevitable. She was still new at the job, and if the principal expected the new junior English teacher at the lecture with the rest of the staff there was no help for it. She would just have to bite the bullet and turn up.

On the evening of the lecture Rosanna asked one of the prefects to reserve a seat for her in the back row, and just before seven took her place just as Dr Marian Lonsdale, a handsome woman in her forties, resplendent tonight in her academic robes, walked onto the stage. She told the girls how lucky they were to have the pleasure of listening to Mr Ewen Fraser, especially those girls doing History and English A levels.

Ewen Fraser walked on stage to a round of applause which grew wild with enthusiasm once the older girls caught sight of him. His hair was newly cut for once, by someone who was good at the job, too, thought Rosanna, her heart contracting. He wore a formal dark suit and gleaming white shirt, and smiled at the assembled audience in a way which won them over instantly. Ewen, thought Rosanna bitterly, was having his usual effect on her sex, young and old. She slid down in her seat, glad she was hidden behind some of the taller members of the Upper Sixth.

Ewen was just as good a speaker as Rosanna expected. He spoke easily and fluently, with very little reference to notes, giving the girls a clear idea of his way of writing a book, the research and long, disciplined hours of labour it involved. From there he went on to the history aspect of his writing, and discussed the far-reaching influences of war. His audience sat rapt, with no fidgeting for the entire time he spoke, and after an enthusiastic ovation at the end of his speech several girls asked eager, intelligent questions which Ewen answered with obvious pleasure in their interest.

Dr Lonsdale brought the session to a close by asking the head of the English department to offer a vote of thanks to Mr Fraser, then she took him off to her study for refreshments.

Rosanna was on duty with Jane Rowlands afterwards, to wait while the girls were collected by their parents.

'Right,' said Jane, when the last car had gone. 'Let's have some coffee. I told them to keep some buns for us.'

'I ought to get home—' began Rosanna.

'I'll give you a lift in the car,' said Jane firmly. 'Come on.'

Rosanna found her colleagues discussing Ewen Fraser with loud animation in the staff-room. She drank down two cups of coffee in quick succession, but the caffeine merely put her more on edge. She longed to get away, but couldn't see how to escape without giving offence to kind, friendly Jane.

None of the teaching staff seemed in any hurry to get home, and Rosanna discovered why when Dr Lonsdale appeared soon after, ushering Ewen Fraser before her. Introductions were made all round, Ewen perfectly at ease in the room full of women.

'And here's Rosanna Carey, our newest recruit to the English department,' said Dr Lonsdale eventually, a twinkle in her eye. 'But of course you know that already, Mr Fraser.' She turned to the room at large. 'Rosanna was lucky enough to help Mr Fraser with his research during the summer.'

'Hello again,' said Ewen pleasantly as all eyes turned on the new junior English teacher. 'How are you, Rosanna?'

She smiled brightly. 'Very well, thank you. I enjoyed your lecture.'

'I'm glad.' He moved on to meet Jane, and a few minutes later left with the principal and Rosanna was thrown to the lions as her colleagues clustered round, demanding information about her work for the author.

'You kept that pretty quiet, Miss Dark Horse!' accused Jane on the way home.

'Dr Lonsdale knew because she asked how I'd been filling in my time since my last teaching job. But I felt I was too much the new girl to go in for name-dropping with the rest of you.' Rosanna shrugged casually. 'Anyway, I did my part of the work in London, while he wrote in his place in the country.'

'So you never saw much of him, then?'

'No, not really,' said Rosanna, glad that the short journey gave Jane no opportunity for more questions.

Rosanna felt unutterably weary as she went down the stairs to the flat. She unlocked the door, hoping that Louise wasn't in a talkative mood, then stood rigid, staring in outrage at the man waiting for her.

'What are you doing here?'

'Your friend let me in,' said Ewen.

'Where is she?' demanded Rosanna fiercely, brushing past him, but Ewen barred her way.

'In her room. But don't rush in after her, please. She didn't want to let me in, but I persuaded her I had something important to say to you.'

Rosanna suddenly reached the end of her tether. The entire day had been a nightmare of tension, and to find Ewen here at the end of it put paid to her self-control.

'I don't want to hear it,' she spat at him, trembling with anger. 'I'm amazed you can show your face in here.'

Ewen frowned. 'I admit we parted on unfriendly terms, Rosanna, but that's why I've come. To put matters right, if I can.'

She glared at him, incensed. 'Unfriendly terms! That's the understatement of the year. Did you honestly think I'd even want to breathe the same air, you—you pervert?'

'Pervert?' Ewen advanced on her, suddenly as angry as she. 'What the hell are you talking about? I admit I jumped to conclusions about the pregnancy, and there were one or two things I didn't make clear—'

'Oh, you made yourself clear all right,' she said with passion.

'No, I damn well didn't,' he retorted. 'A stupid mistake for an author, I know, but I used the wrong words.'

'On the contrary, they were very much to the point!'

They stood glaring at each other, then Rosanna pointed to the door, which still stood open. 'Just go.'

'Not until I've had my say!' he said tightly.

She ground her teeth in fury. 'Get on with it, then. I'm tired. Though thank heavens I don't have to work tomorrow. Otherwise, courtesy of my link with you, I'd be the main topic of conversation in the staffroom.'

'It didn't come from me,' he said curtly.

'I know,' she admitted grudgingly. 'Dr Lonsdale had a chat with me the day I started and I mentioned I'd done some temping for Charlie Clayton—and you.' She frowned. 'Is that why she asked you to speak?'

Ewen eyed her warily. 'Actually, no. I volunteered. If I can just close the door, I'll explain.'

Rosanna crossed the room and closed the door herself, then stood against it, arms folded. 'So?'

'Beaumont's on the list of schools my editor's looking at for her daughter. You remember Harriet, of course?' he added, raising an eyebrow. 'When she went to the school for an interview with Dr Lonsdale I told her to drop a hint. I was asked to give a talk at my old school not so long ago, which gave me the idea.' Ewen looked at her levelly. 'I hope you're proud of what you reduce me to, Rosanna. I couldn't see any other way of getting to you.'

'And you know why,' she said icily.

'Actually,' he said with exaggerated patience, 'I don't. And I take strong exception to the word ''pervert'', Rosanna. What the hell was all that about?'

'What else would you call a man who seduces schoolgirls?' she threw at him.

Ewen stared at her, thunderstruck. *What?*

'You may have forgotten that day at the cottage, but I haven't.' She shuddered. 'I still can't think about it without wanting to throw up.'

He stood very still, a white line around his mouth. 'I'm sorry you remember it that way.

For me what happened between us was a rare, beautiful thing—'

'I'm not talking about that!' she said desperately. 'I mean the *last* time I was there. When you sent me packing.'

'I did *what*?' he demanded, astonished.

'You mean, you've forgotten?' She gave a mirthless bark of laughter. 'I haven't.'

'Rosanna,' he said very quietly. 'Until that day at the book signing, I hadn't laid eyes on you since we said goodbye in this room.'

'You didn't actually *see* me on the day I'm talking about,' she said bitterly. 'Sally answered the door, stark naked under one of your dressing gowns. She went up to your bedroom to tell you I was there. I heard you talking to her, then she strutted back to tell me—with enormous relish—that you were too busy to see me.'

'*What?*' Ewen swore colourfully and at length. 'The spiteful little devil! I don't know who the hell she had up there but it certainly wasn't me. She's fifteen years old, for God's sake.'

Rosanna came away from the door. 'You weren't there?'

'Damn right I wasn't. I make sure I'm out of the house when Sally's cleaning. I'm not a total fool, no matter what you think.' His eyes narrowed. 'It must have been when I went back up to London for a meeting with Harriet. I spent a couple of nights with my parents for once. Bob Todd told me Sally cleaned up while I was away.' His lips twisted with disgust. 'I'd like to know who the hell she had in my bed, the little witch.'

As long as it wasn't Ewen Rosanna didn't care a jot who it was. She looked at him in silence, feeling a great knot of ice dissolve inside her. 'Want some coffee?' she asked at last.

Ewen let out a deep breath, his taut face relaxing slightly. 'Yes, please. Do you have any of those biscuits you keep giving me? I haven't eaten yet.'

'Neither have I.' She smiled diffidently. 'I could make sandwiches.'

His eyes locked with hers. 'First, Rosanna, tell me you believe me. Where Sally's concerned.'

'Yes, I do.' She shrugged. 'It would be so easy to prove, anyway.'

'I suppose it would.' He gave her the familiar, lopsided smile. 'Do you think you should let your friend out of her room?'

Rosanna clapped a hand to her forehead. 'I forgot about Louise!'

Once Louise had been persuaded out of hiding, there was no more opportunity for private talk. But Rosanna and Ewen were so obviously not at daggers drawn any more, a deeply relieved Louise helped make sandwiches and coffee, shared them, then got up the moment she'd finished eating.

'I must wash my hair or I'll never get to bed.' She smiled. 'Goodnight, Ewen. I'm glad I've met you properly at last. I hope I'll see you again.'

'I hope you will too,' he assured her, and looked at Rosanna. 'Put in a good word for me.'

'I don't think I need to,' Louise told him happily.

'Was she right?' asked Ewen when she'd gone.

'I suppose she was,' admitted Rosanna. 'Now I know you weren't in bed with Sally I feel less hostile, certainly.' She yawned. 'Sorry. This has been a very tiring day.'

Ewen subjected her to a long, appraising scrutiny that Rosanna endured unwillingly, conscious of her unadorned navy wool dress and tightly coiled hair.

'You've lost more weight,' he said at last.

'I run to school and back every day.'

'You'll soon have to give that a miss now the nights are darker.'

'I know.' She eyed him questioningly. 'You had other things you wanted to say?'

'Yes, but not tonight. You're too tired.' Ewen stood erect. 'And I'd like my name cleared before I say any of them. Rosanna, come down to the cottage with me tomorrow. Please. I'd like to confront Sally in person.'

The idea appealed strongly, for more than one reason. Rosanna pretended to think it over then nodded, knowing she was saying yes to a great deal more than a trip to the country. She wasn't quite sure what, but if it involved Ewen it was enough for now, whatever it was.

'Thank you, I'd like that. I haven't been any-where much since term started.'

Ewen got up. 'I'll pick you up at ten, then. We can have lunch in the village pub again.'

'Sounds good,' she said, brisk to hide her tension as she wondered if he'd kiss her good-night.

But at the door Ewen merely thanked her for supper, and said goodnight without even shaking her hand. Even so Rosanna went to bed in a happier frame of mind than she'd known for months.

She woke next morning feeling as though a great black cloud had been blown away from her life. The weather reflected her mood, sunny and unusually warm for the season, and she dressed in jeans and deck shoes, pulled a plain white cotton T-shirt over her head, and left her hair loose to frame a face glowing with antic-ipation for the day ahead.

'Good morning. You look—different,' said Ewen, when she opened the door to him. He was wearing the light tweed jacket and jeans of their first meeting, the same look of startled appreciation on his face.

'I slept well,' she said cheerfully. 'Want some coffee? Or would you rather not leave the car abandoned out there?'

He grinned. 'Got it in one.'

Rosanna called goodbye through Louise's bedroom door, picked up her tote bag and navy blazer, and went off with Ewen into the bright October morning, feeling vastly different from any morning since she'd last seen him.

Cocooned against the wind by the Morgan's hood, Rosanna enjoyed the journey a great deal more than her own trip to Long Ashley.

'I was a lot slower getting to this point than you,' she commented as they turned off the motorway. 'My mother's car protests if I try to speed.'

'I wondered how you got here,' said Ewen as they began winding through the familiar Gloucestershire landscape. 'Long Ashley's not very accessible by public transport.'

'Does Sally know you're coming today?' asked Rosanna curiously.

Ewen shook his head, his mouth tightening ominously. 'I made sure she'd be working in the house, but I said I was probably coming tomorrow.'

Rosanna was almost sorry for the girl, until they turned in at the cottage entrance. Memories of her last visit came flooding back, and Ewen sensed her recoil, holding her hand tightly as they walked up the gravel path to the door. He strode ahead of Rosanna into the hall then stood, arms folded, to confront the girl who came running down the stairs. Sally stopped dead in her tracks at the sight of them, her eyes like saucers.

'Hello, Sally,' he said menacingly.

The girl swallowed, her eyes darting guiltily in Rosanna's direction, then back in frightened appeal at Ewen. 'Mr Fraser—I didn't know you were coming today. I haven't finished yet.'

'No problem. I'm taking Miss Carey down to the pub for lunch. You can finish while we're out. In the meantime, come through to the kitchen, please.'

The girl eyed Rosanna in trepidation, then scuttled through past Ewen, casting another scared look at his forbidding face. Ewen ushered Rosanna ahead of him then stood in the kitchen doorway, his brows drawn together in a daunting scowl.

'Miss Carey's given me an account of her last visit here, Sally. Why did you lie?'

Sally burst into noisy tears, knuckling her eyes like a child. 'I'm ever so sorry. *Please* don't tell my dad, Mr Fraser. He'd kill me!'

'I doubt that. And stop that noise, please.' Ewen tore off a length of kitchen towel, and handed it to her. 'Now tell me who you had here, and why the devil you told Miss Carey it was me.'

'It was my boyfriend,' she sobbed, and blew her nose, hiccuping.

'Does he know how old you are?' demanded Ewen.

'Course he does. He's in the same class in school,' said Sally indignantly.

Rosanna avoided Ewen's eyes, her ribs aching with the effort to control her mirth.

'I see,' he said severely. 'It doesn't excuse the fact that you invited some stranger into my bed—'

'He's not a stranger, Mr Fraser, he's my boyfriend!'

'I don't care who it was, you were out of order!' barked Ewen. 'And what the hell were you playing at when you told Miss Carey it was me?'

At which Sally began sobbing so hysterically, Rosanna asked Ewen to leave them alone together. 'You're frightening her.'

'I should damn well hope so!' he snorted, and strode from the room in disgust.

'Now then, Sally,' said Rosanna, in her best schoolmarm tone, 'stop that noise. At once, please. Wash your face with cold water.'

Sally obeyed blindly, splashing her face so liberally, her hair was wet at the front when she raised her streaming face from the kitchen sink. Rosanna handed her a towel and waited until the girl mopped herself dry.

'Right then, Sally. Confession time. Why did you lie to me?'

'It was Wayne's idea. But I was jealous, too,' said the girl miserably. 'You dress too plain, but you're so pretty, miss, and I—well, I—'

'You like Mr Fraser,' said Rosanna gently.

The girl blushed to the roots of her hair. 'Don't tell him, miss, *please*,' she implored. 'Wayne said to lie to make you go away, because you caught us together.' She sighed tragically. 'Do you think Ewen—Mr Fraser—will sack me now? I was saving up so hard.'

'What were you saving for, Sally?'

'The school trip. They're going to France, and my dad said I could go if I paid a little bit towards it out of my wages.' The girl's red eyes blazed with entreaty. 'If I get the sack Dad won't let me go on the trip. And *Wayne's* going,' she added with a wail.

Rosanna promised to put in a good word with Mr Fraser, but in turn extracted several promises from the penitent Sally, who by that stage was ready to agree to anything.

'Sally was very chastened. What did you say to her?' said Ewen soon after as they strolled to the pub for lunch.

'I gave her a lecture. Not that it did much good. She hasn't a clue about the harm she caused.'

'No,' he said grimly, and took her hand in his, clasping it tightly. 'I thought I'd lost you for good.'

'You can understand how I felt, surely?'

'Of course I do—now!' He turned to look at her. 'But did you really think I'd sent you away, Rosanna?'

'The evidence was against you.' She thrust back her hair with her free hand. 'Don't let's talk about that any more. One thing you can be sure of, anyway. Your house will be gleaming when we get back, today and for the foreseeable future. Sally was terrified you'd give her the sack.'

'If she'd been anyone else's daughter I would have,' said Ewen grimly. 'Bob would take his belt to her if he knew the half of it.'

'Sally's well aware of that. She'll be good as gold from now on. Except where Wayne's concerned, I'm afraid.'

'Who the blazes is Wayne?'

'The boyfriend.' Rosanna giggled suddenly. 'I gave her some pretty frank advice about her relationship with the enterprising Wayne. I won't make you blush with the details.'

'As long as she keeps him away from my bed she can do what she likes!' said Ewen, laughing.

This time they ate large portions of chicken and ham pie, served with fresh vegetables supplied, said Ewen, straight-faced, by Bob Todd.

Rosanna gave a choke of laughter, and put down her laden fork. 'Out of your garden by any chance?'

'Probably.' Ewen grinned, and sat back with a sigh when he'd cleared his plate. 'After all the drama back there I was starving.'

'I was ready to eat a horse myself,' she admitted.

'Which wouldn't do you any harm,' he said, eyeing her. 'You're too thin, Rosanna.'

She pushed her plate away and sat back, arms folded as she looked at him. 'Does that mean you don't fancy me any more?'

His eyes kindled. 'You know damn well it doesn't, but I'd rather not discuss it here.'

'Let's go and discuss it at home, then,' she said casually, and Ewen leapt to his feet with alacrity.

'You said "home",' he remarked as they walked back.

'Figure of speech.'

'I hope you meant it.' He took her hand in his. 'Talking of which, this is as good a time as any, I suppose.'

'For what?'

'To say what I came to say the other night. But once I heard about Sally I felt I needed total exoneration before I brought the subject up again.' His fingers tightened on hers. 'My mother requested my presence not so long ago. She wanted a little talk with me, she said. An opening which made me nervous, big strong chap though I am.'

Rosanna looked up at him, intrigued. 'What did she say?'

'She informed me that she was very taken with your parents when they came to lunch, and couldn't understand why I was letting you slip through my fingers, so to speak, when it was obvious to everyone, my grandmother included, that I was crazy about you.'

'Oh.'

'Yes. Oh. So I told her I'd asked and been rejected. And then she enquired as to the exact nature of my question and showed me the error of my ways. I'd talked about wanting you and moving in together—'

'Exactly. It smacked of the temporary to an old-fashioned girl like me.'

Ewen eyed her ruefully as they turned in through the gate. 'Then I must have got my syntax snarled. I meant that life is short and we can't tell how much of it we're allotted, but what there is of it I want to spend with you. Until death us do part.'

'Oh,' said Rosanna again, her voice unsteady this time.

'Can't you say anything but "oh"?' he demanded.

Rosanna turned to him in the gleaming, immaculate hall. 'I could say "yes", if asked the right question.'

The sudden light in Ewen's eyes almost dazzled her.

'I've got a few,' he assured her. 'First, will you marry me, second, will you stay to supper, or better still—because I assume you need to be back for school on Monday—will you stay here with me until Sunday night?'

Rosanna was so overcome with emotion for a minute, she clasped her hands together and put her head on one side, pretending to think it over.

'Well?' he said impatiently.

'Yes to all three,' she said at last, and he hauled her into his arms and kissed her until her head reeled.

'I still haven't put things completely straight,' he said when he raised his head a little. 'I said want, and it's true. You know how much. But I love you, Rosanna. You, not a ghost. When you chose David over me—'

'I kept on trying to explain about that,' she interrupted crossly, pushing him away. 'So listen. Properly, this time. David did come to tell me he was marrying someone else. But it made no difference. Because I was going to tell him I was, too. Only he got in first. Although,' she reminded him, eyes flashing, 'you never seriously mentioned marriage!'

'Fool that I am, I thought I had.' Ewen grabbed her by the shoulders and shook her slightly. 'So I wasn't second choice after all?'

'I never had a choice at all, once I met you.' She smiled at him ruefully. 'Because of David I tried to fight against it, but it was useless. Otherwise, Mr Fraser,' she added primly, 'I would not have consented to share your bed.'

Ewen breathed in deeply, cast a look at the stairs, then shook his head. 'No,' he said firmly. 'We are going to spend the day watching sport on television, or playing board games, or reading, or just talking, making plans. I don't just want bed, darling. I just want to be with you, savouring every minute of our time together, whatever we're doing.'

They went into the sitting room and Rosanna smiled invitingly as she curled up on the sofa. 'We broke up for half term yesterday. I don't go back until Monday week.'

Ewen sat down beside her and hauled her onto his lap, kissing her for a long, breathless interval. 'Stay here with me until then.'

'My mother's expecting me for lunch tomorrow, and I haven't brought any clothes,' she said huskily, rubbing her cheek against his.

'Ring your mother and postpone lunch until next Sunday instead, and tell her I'm coming with you, to ask your father for his daughter's hand in the time-honoured way. Though I want the rest of you too,' he pointed out, kissing the hollow behind her ear. 'The clothes don't matter. You can borrow something of mine. Or I'll take you shopping in Cheltenham.'

'OK,' she said simply.

Ewen sat very still, then turned her face up to his. 'You mean that?'

She nodded. 'Don't you think we've wasted too much time already?'

'Too right I do,' he said, with a deep breath of thankfulness. 'Several bloody awful weeks of it. God, I've missed you, my darling.'

Rosanna hugged him hard. 'I've missed you, too.'

It was much later that night, after keeping steadfastly to his programme, when Ewen took her upstairs to bed at last.

'Don't worry,' he said as he closed the door behind them. 'The bedlinen's been changed several times since Wayne's occupation.'

Rosanna giggled. 'That's a relief! By the way, have you noticed how sparkling the entire house is? Sally must have worked her fingers to the bone.' Her smile faded as she saw the single, perfect rosebud in a crystal vase on the bedside table. 'Roses? At this time of the year?'

He looked at it in surprise. 'There are still a few in the garden, but I didn't put it there.'

'I think it's Sally's olive branch.' Rosanna smiled at him. 'Highly appropriate.'

'Only because it's beautiful. Like you.' Ewen took her in his arms. 'It was always you, Rosanna, right from the first moment on your doorstep. No ghost. Just you.'

She leaned against him, savouring the moment of tenderness and peace before the urgency began. As it would, she knew. For both of them. 'I know. Besides, I only *look* like my grandmother. I could never have been noble, like Rose.'

Ewen's arms tightened. 'In what way?'

Rosanna looked up into his intent, possessive face. 'David's fit and healthy and all in one piece—'

'And a pretty hefty piece at that!'

'Don't be rude. What I'm trying to say is that Rose kept her promise to marry Gerald Rivers, my grandfather. But I couldn't have done it. I'm glad David's found someone else. But even if he hadn't it wouldn't have made any difference. I could never have married him—or anyone else—once I found you.'

Ewen let out a long, unsteady breath, and kissed her with a tenderness that brought tears to her eyes as she smiled up at him.

'And while I'm in confessing mood,' she went on, 'I might as well tell you why I came to the cottage that day.'

'To kiss and make up, I hope,' he said, rubbing his cheek against hers.

'A bit more than that.' She moved back a little so she could look up into his eyes. 'Actually I came to accept your terms, Ewen Fraser.'

He frowned. 'What terms?'

'I was so unhappy without you I was ready to accept your offer.'

Ewen's eyes glittered. 'You mean you were actually willing to live in sin with me, Miss Carey?'

'Since you were so allergic to marriage, Mr Fraser, what else could I do?'

'So we abandoned our previous stands almost simultaneously?' he said in amazement, then pulled her to him with sudden ferocity. 'Now I know you love me.'

'Did you ever doubt it?' she said against his shirt.

'Damn right I did, once I laid eyes on Dr Norton.'

She gave a muffled laugh. 'Let's not bring all that up again.'

Ewen turned her face up to his. 'What shall we do instead?'

When her eyes gave him her answer he crushed her to him then took her to bed, and it was in the early hours of the morning, long after they'd celebrated their reunion with passionate thanksgiving, that Ewen told her he'd rewritten the ending of his book.

Rosanna propped herself on an elbow to look at him in the soft, muted lamplight. 'You mean your heroine didn't make the sacrifice after all?'

'Oh, yes, she made it. She parts from her lover in anguish and marries the disabled fiancé.' Ewen reached up and pulled her down to him, settling her comfortably against his shoulder. 'But he dies three years later, and she meets the lover by chance in Hyde Park one day, when she's out walking with the son she named for him.'

'*And?*' demanded Rosanna.

Ewen kissed her. 'When you think of the passionately physical relationship between Rose and Harry, and the times they lived in, don't you think it's a bit of a miracle there was no child born of it?'

She nodded, her eyes glowing with sudden comprehension. 'So in your book there was. The child she named for him actually *was* his.'

'Right. So they get married and he adopts the son, who will feature in my next book— Why are you laughing?'

'*That's* why you made the child his, Ewen Fraser—you needed the character for your next novel!'

'True,' he agreed. 'But quite apart from that I had this compulsion to write a happy ending.'

'I'm glad,' said Rosanna fervently. 'Everyone loves a happy ending.' She shivered and slid further down into his arms. 'We came horribly close to missing ours.'

'Not a chance!' Ewen held her close with sudden urgency. 'Fate had us marked out for each other from the start.'

'Perhaps that's what my grandmother meant,' said Rosanna breathlessly.

'When?'

'She said I should read the diary and the letters when the time was right. And it was. An hour after I finished reading them you appeared on the doorstep!'

'Struck dumb at the sight of you. I thought Rose's photograph had come to life.' Ewen leaned over her possessively, his hand tracing the line of her cheek. 'Then I took a second look and knew exactly who you were.'

'Who?' she whispered.

'My destiny,' said Ewen, and turned out the light.